BANDETTE™

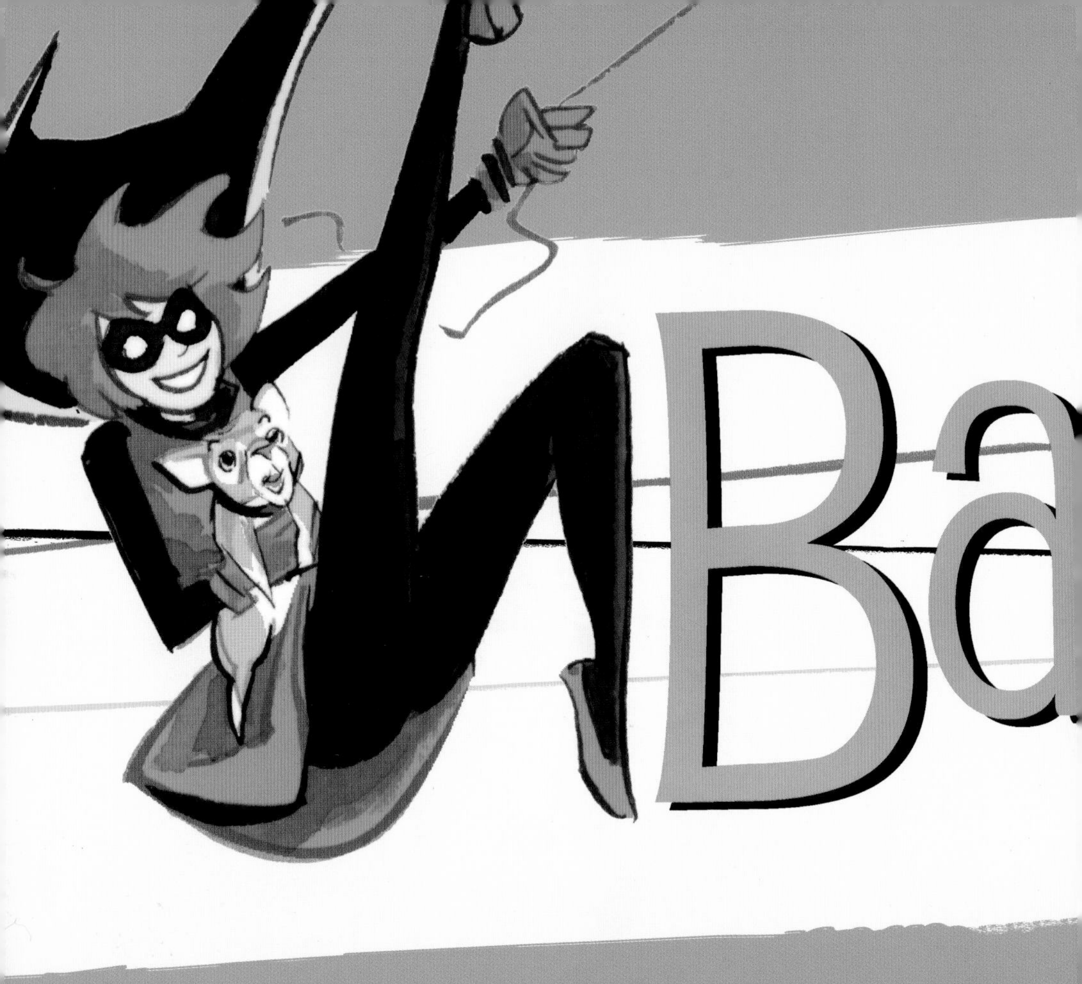
Ba

NDETTE™

in THE HOUSE OF THE GREEN MASK

Story by PAUL TOBIN

Art by COLLEEN COOVER

Foreword by KURT BUSIEK

DARK HORSE BOOKS

President and Publisher MIKE RICHARDSON
Editor SHANTEL LAROCQUE

HARDCOVER EDITION

Designer JACK THOMAS

Digital Art Technician CHRISTINA MCKENZIE

PAPERBACK EDITION

Associate Editor BRETT ISRAEL

Designer KATHLEEN BARNETT

Digital Art Technician ANN GRAY

NEIL HANKERSON Executive Vice President • TOM WEDDLE Chief Financial Officer • RANDY STRADLEY Vice President of Publishing • NICK McWHORTER Chief Business Development Officer • DALE LaFOUNTAIN Chief Information Officer • MATT PARKINSON Vice President of Marketing • VANESSA TODD-HOLMES Vice President of Production and Scheduling • MARK BERNARDI Vice President of Book Trade and Digital Sales • KEN LIZZI General Counsel • DAVE MARSHALL Editor in Chief • DAVEY ESTRADA Editorial Director • CHRIS WARNER Senior Books Editor • CARY GRAZZINI Director of Specialty Projects • LIA RIBACCHI Art Director • MATT DRYER Director of Digital Art and Prepress • MICHAEL GOMBOS Senior Director of Licensed Publications • KARI YADRO Director of Custom Programs • KARI TORSON Director of International Licensing • SEAN BRICE Director of Trade Sales

Published by Dark Horse Books
A division of Dark Horse Comics LLC
10956 SE Main Street
Milwaukie, Oregon 97222

DarkHorse.com

Library of Congress Cataloging-in-Publication Data

Names: Tobin, Paul, 1965- author. | Coover, Colleen, artist.
Title: The house of the green mask / story by Paul Tobin ; art by Colleen Coover.
Description: First paperback edition. | Milwaukie, OR : Dark Horse Books, 2020. | Series: Bandette ; volume 3 | Audience: Ages 12+ | Summary: "The greatest thief in all the lands, uncovers the greatest of all mysteries: a clue to the location of the legendary House of the Green Mask! But the sinister Voice has set his sights on the same treasure and sent a deadly assassin after the same secrets! Worse, he's stolen the one thing dearest to Bandette's heart. Now, she's after revenge! (And also chocolate.)"– Provided by publisher.
Identifiers: LCCN 2020004724 | ISBN 9781506719252 (trade paperback)
Subjects: LCSH: Graphic novels. | CYAC: Graphic novels. | Robbers and outlaws–Fiction.
Classification: LCC PZ7.7.T62 Ho 2020 | DDC 741.5/973–dc23
LC record available at https://lccn.loc.gov/2020004724

First hardcover edition: October 2016
Hardcover ISBN: 978-1-50670-219-3
First paperback edition: May 2021
Trade Paperback ISBN: 978-1-50671-925-2

10 9 8 7 6 5 4 3 2 1
Printed in China

THIS TIME IT'S PERCIVAL

First, a digression. But don't worry, I'll get to *Bandette*.

Here's a secret of the writing trade (and, I expect, the arting trade, too): It's easier to learn from bad stuff than from good.

If you read a story that doesn't work, it's easier to articulate why it doesn't work—even if you've never run into that problem before—than to explain why a good story works. With a bad story, or even a good but faulty one, you find yourself thinking, "Oh, that didn't work because the bad guys needed to be scarier." Or the hero needed to seem cooler before events started undercutting him. Or the narrator needed to be more sympathetic. Or less sympathetic. Or, you know, whatever. You teach yourself what works and what doesn't—at least for you—by diagnosing the faults in a work and how you could fix them.

But a good story just *works*. It's in balance, it sets things up naturally, so you don't know you're being set up—and when the dominoes fall, they fall with precision and impact, and you just sit there and admire it.

That's what I do with *Bandette* (see, told you I'd get here). It's a tour de force by two creators working in harmony, playing off one another perfectly, knowing when to be daffy and when to be serious, how to build sympathy and pay it off, how to build characters that charm and threaten and yearn and stomp, steal treasures and steal your heart. And I just sit there and think, "How the hell did they do that?!" And then smile and turn the page and enjoy the show.

But here I am writing about it, so I'd better have more than that. And I think I do.

Here's why I think *Bandette* works so well: *Love and style.*

Okay, I hear you say, I get that. Bandette's all about love and style. She'll tell you that herself!

But that's not what I'm saying. I mean for Colleen and Paul, it's love and style. That's what they put into it. That's why it's so good.

The two of them love comics, movies, TV shows, toys, and more. There's all this stuff out there in the world that delights them, that they hold close to their hearts. And that's what *Bandette*'s made of.

I don't have to tell you (not if you've read either of the earlier volumes, at least) that *Bandette* is built out of a love for Audrey Hepburn and *To Catch a Thief* and *Tintin* and *The Pink Panther* and more. But it's not just the obvious stuff. There's also a healthy dollop of *Dennis the Menace* comics and Jaime Hernandez, some Roy Crane and Harvey Kurtzman, daffy superhero comics . . . and the list goes on. Sure, the Urchins are inspired by the Baker Street Irregulars, but also by every gang of kids that helped a hero, every *Ocean's 11*–style human clockwork that impeded the heavies and let the good guys slip through. Monsieur comes from a long tradition of master thieves—all of them, I'm sure, gently despairing at this bright, sparrow-like upstart. B. D. Belgique, Margot, Pimento . . .

. . . Paul and Colleen made them all with love, from what they love, piling object of affection upon object of affection until the stories are stuffed with treasure. And then, from all these ingredients, they make something new. And they do it with style, giddily building sweet confections that'll let you love all these ideas, all these characters, as much as they do.

You can feel that love, sense that they're having a blast making these stories. They get to be charming, touching, funny—and it regularly amazes me how well Colleen and Paul can switch back and forth from whimsy to adventure to comedy to incisive character moments to romance to . . . well, whatever they want to, it seems.

That's style. That's craft. That's skill.

And love and style together? That's magic. And that's what you get with *Bandette*.

But you know that, if you're a regular reader. And if not, you're about to find out. So go ahead. Get ready to smile. Now turn the page, and enjoy the show . . .

—Kurt Busiek

Previously...

BANDETTE, thief of HEARTS as well as TREASURE, has charmed and delighted the ENTIRE WORLD!

She is AIDED in her adventures by the URCHINS, her troop of FAITHFUL FRIENDS!

Even the SPECIAL POLICE will GRUDGINGLY turn to Bandette for her help in solving MAJOR CRIMES!

Such BOLD ACTIVITIES cause her to run afoul of the evil organization FINIS and its leader, ABSINTHE!

But while Absinthe schemes to kill BANDETTE, his companion MARGOT secretly plots HIS downfall!

Sharing Margot's information, Bandette and fellow thief MONSIEUR join forces against the odious Absinthe!

Their combined efforts are finally SUCCESSFUL! Monsieur spirits Margot away from the clutches of FINIS...

...and Bandette delivers ABSINTHE to the waiting hands of the LAW!

What new adventures lie ahead?!

And now, MORE BANDETTE!

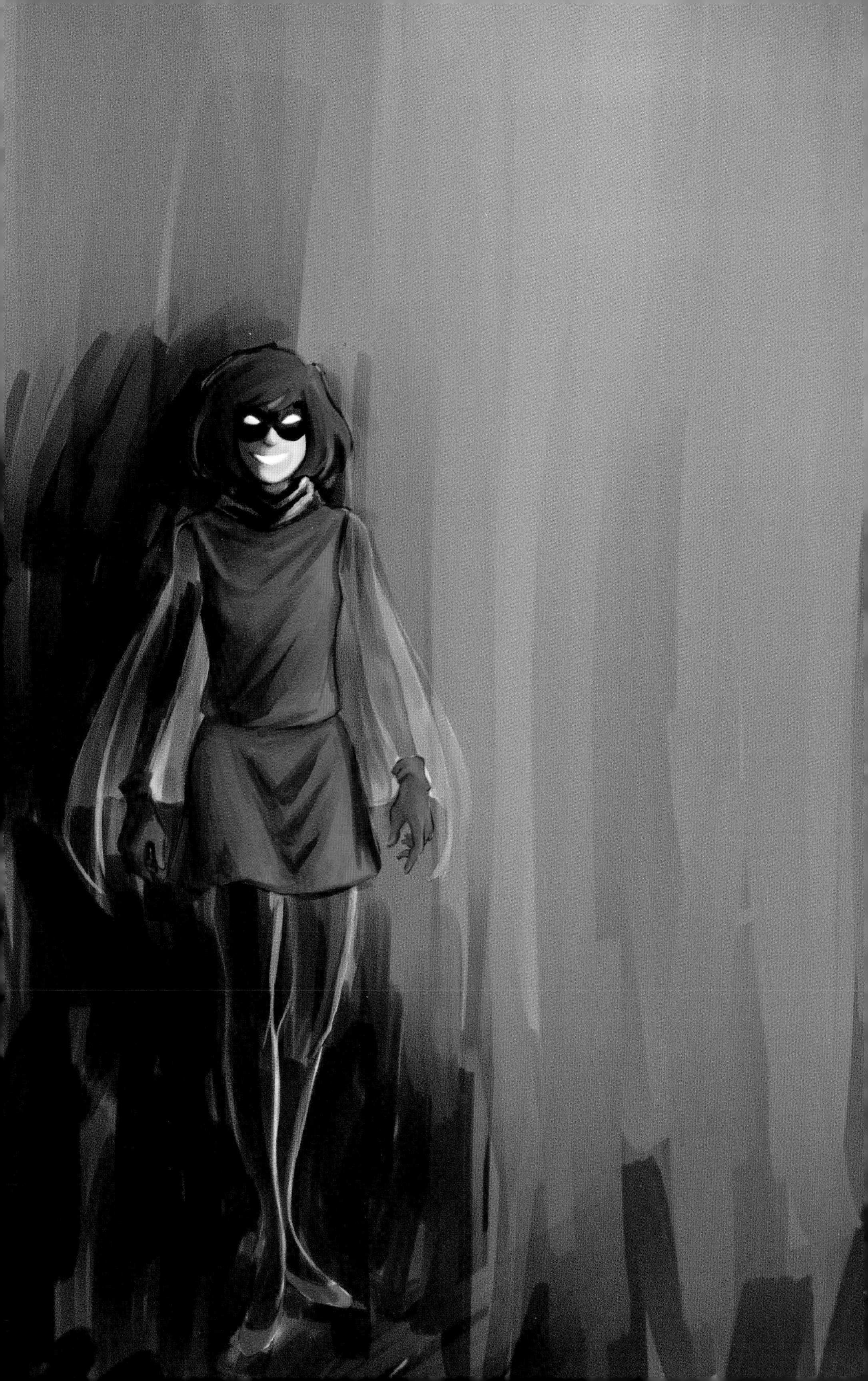

CHAPTER ONE

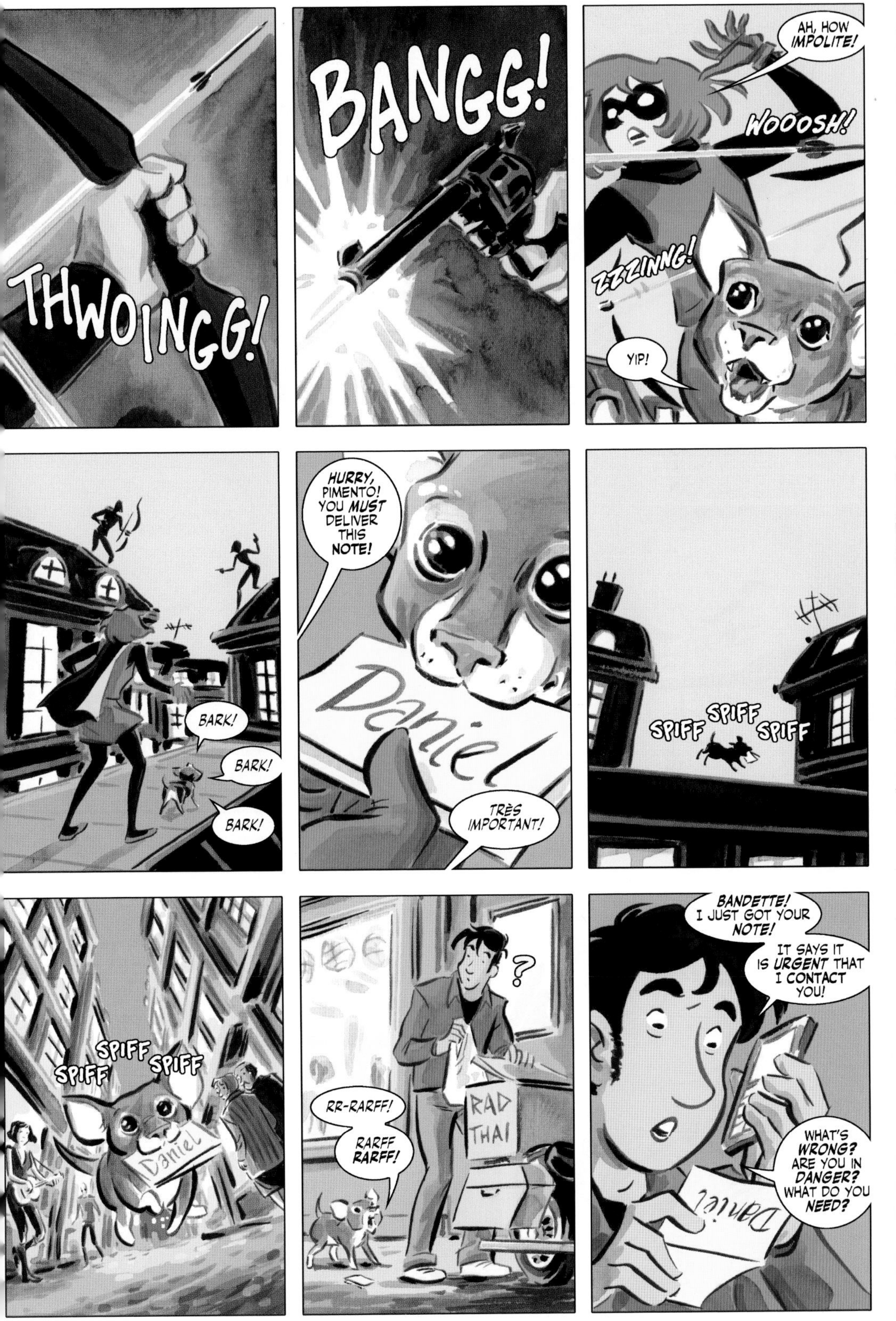
THWOINGG!
BANGG!
AH, HOW IMPOLITE!
WOOOSH!
ZZZINNG!
YIP!
BARK!
BARK!
BARK!
HURRY, PIMENTO! YOU MUST DELIVER THIS NOTE!
Daniel
TRÈS IMPORTANT!
SPIFF SPIFF SPIFF
SPIFF SPIFF SPIFF
Daniel
?
RAD THAI
RR-RARFF!
RARFF RARFF!
BANDETTE! I JUST GOT YOUR NOTE!
IT SAYS IT IS URGENT THAT I CONTACT YOU!
WHAT'S WRONG? ARE YOU IN DANGER? WHAT DO YOU NEED?
Daniel

AHH, *DANIEL!* JUST IN TIME!

IT IS *I,* BANDETTE, THE WORLD'S *GREATEST* THIEF!

FLIP!

HOOOSH!

ZZZINNG!

I AM FIGHTING THE *ELEGANT ASSASSINS!*

"ONE IS A MASTER OF THE *BOW,* WITH SKILLS TO RIVAL THOSE OF THE LEGENDARY *ROBIN HOOD!*"

"AND HIS *TWIN,* THE DEADLY WOMAN KNOWN AS *MADAME REVOLVER,* COULD SHOOT A FLY AT ONE HUNDRED PACES...

"...SHOULD SHE FOR SOME REASON BE *ANGRY* WITH THIS HYPOTHETICAL FLY."

TOGETHER, WE ARE IN A DISPUTE OVER MY CONTINUED EXISTENCE.

OOF!

THUMP!

DO YOU NEED *HELP?* AN *ESCAPE* CAR? OR...AN *ESCAPE* SCOOTER?

I WILL BE THERE IN *MOMENTS!*

AHH, *NO!* NO NO NO.

NONE OF THESE ARE NECESSARY.

THERE IS *ANOTHER MATTER.* AN UPCOMING THEFT OF *GRAVE IMPORTANCE!*

"THERE IS A FILM SHOWING AT THE THEATER TONIGHT.

"A BIOGRAPHY OF THE LEGENDARY *MADAME PRESTO*...FABULIST, MESMERIST, WOMAN OF IMPUDENT MORALS.

Madame Presto!

TONIGHT ONLY!
RECENTLY DISCOVERED FILM BIOGRAPHY OF MADAME PRESTO, GREATEST OF LES MAGICIENS FÉMININS!

"DIGNITARIES ONLY ARE INVITED...

"...FOR THE MYSTERIOUS **MADAME PRESTO** ONCE OWNED THE FABULOUS *MOGUL MUGHAL EMERALD*...

"...WHICH WILL BE ON DISPLAY DURING THIS NIGHT'S **EVENT**."

AND SO, THIS EVENING...

AS THE RARE FILM BIOGRAPHY OF **MADAME PRESTO** IS SHOWING, AND THE GUARDS ARE THEREBY *DISTRACTED*...

THERE WILL BE...

A THEFT!

ZZZINNG!

13

THE PLAN!

"DANIEL, YOU WILL DISGUISE YOURSELF AS THE POPCORN SELLER.

"THE THREE BALLERINAS WILL BE TAKING TICKETS.

"THE USHERS WILL BE DALTON...AND FRECKLES...

"...AND PIMENTO."

AARP!

AARP!   AARP!

DO NOT FAIL TO ATTEND, DANIEL, FOR YOU HAVE THE MOST IMPORTANT PART!

AU REVOIR!

CLICK!

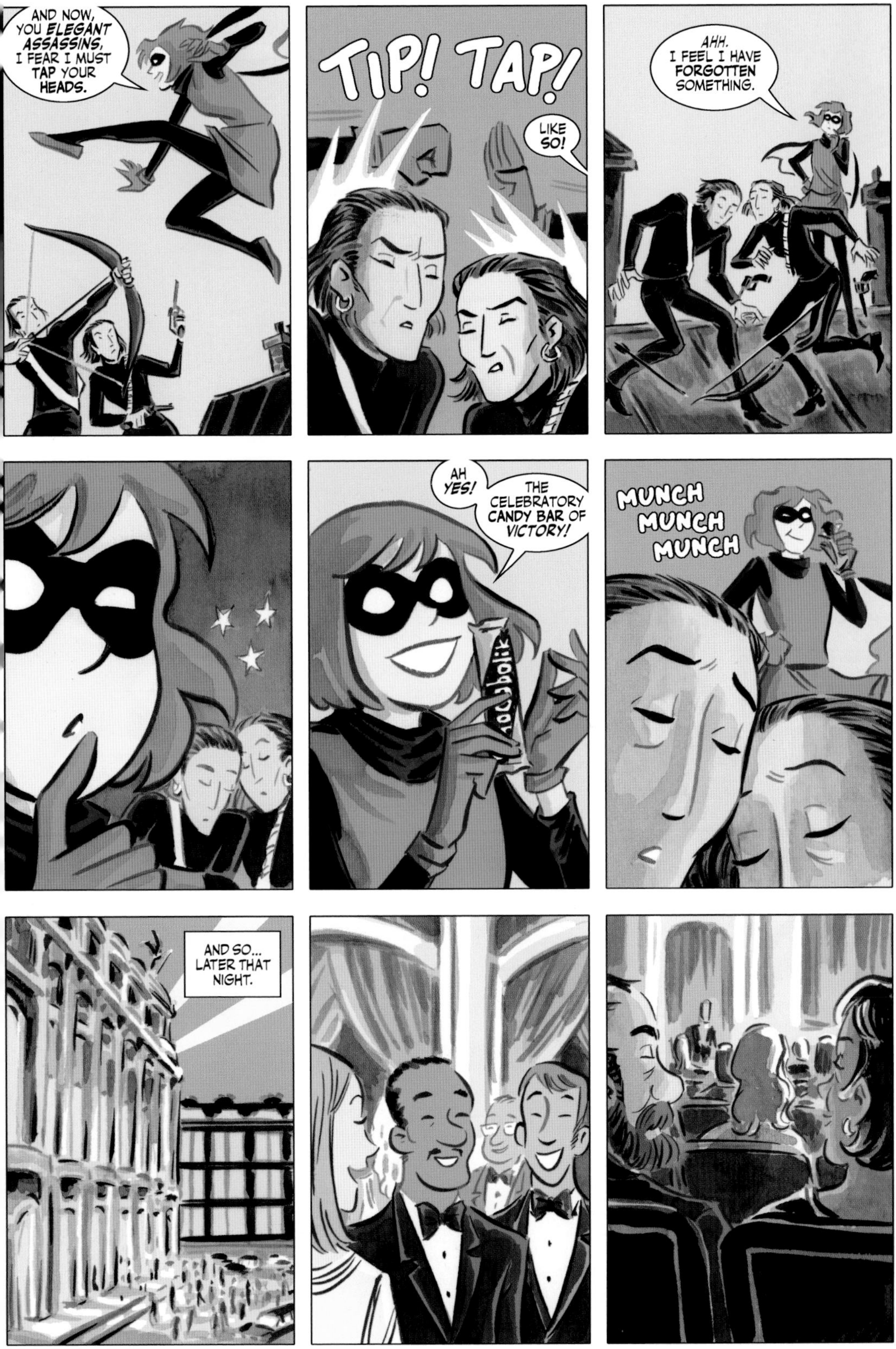
AND NOW, YOU *ELEGANT ASSASSINS,* I FEAR I MUST **TAP YOUR HEADS.**
TIP! TAP!
LIKE SO!
AHH. I FEEL I HAVE **FORGOTTEN** SOMETHING.
AH *YES!*
THE CELEBRATORY **CANDY BAR** OF *VICTORY!*
MUNCH MUNCH MUNCH
AND SO... LATER THAT NIGHT.

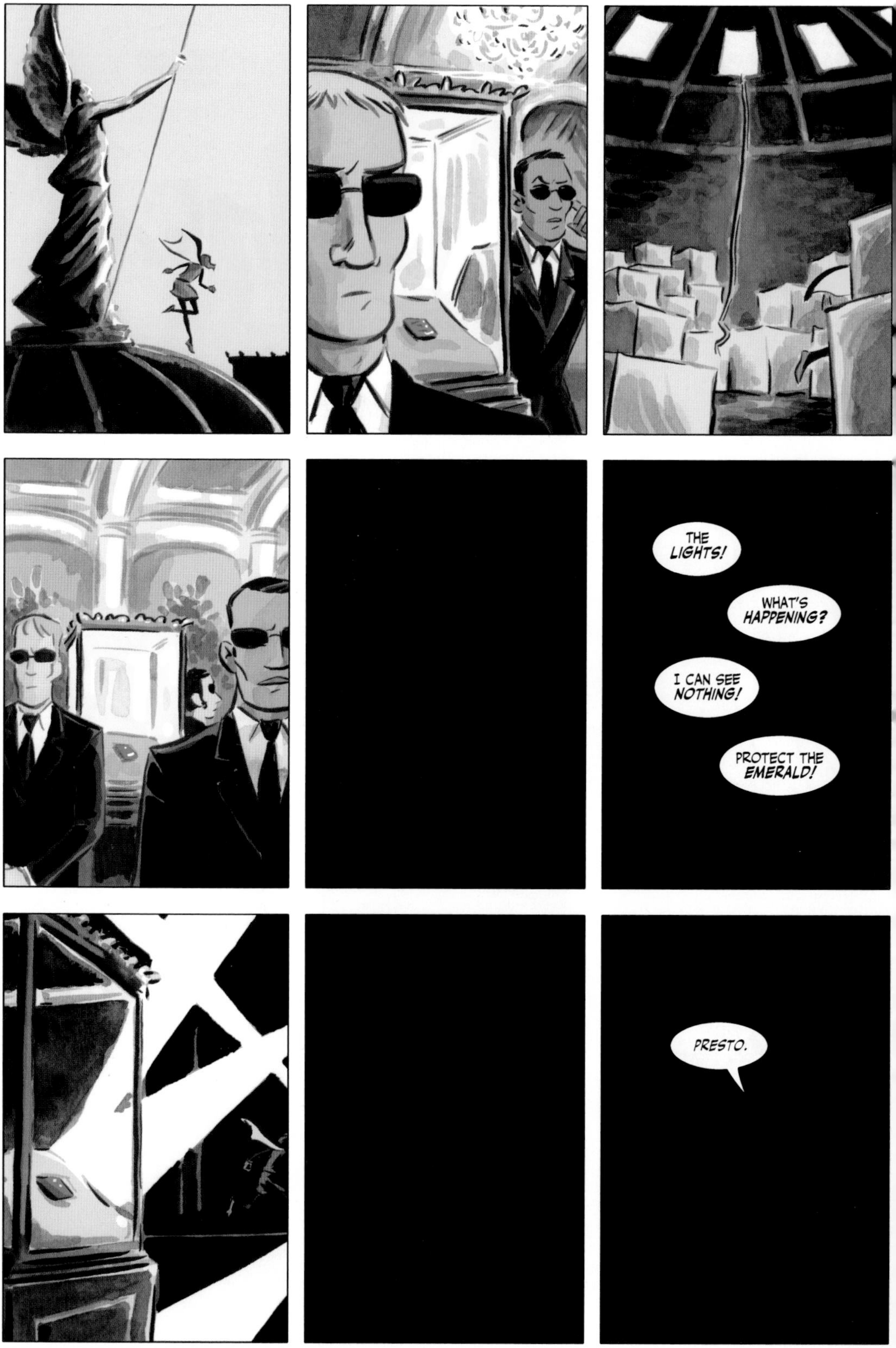
THE LIGHTS!
WHAT'S HAPPENING?
I CAN SEE NOTHING!
PROTECT THE EMERALD!
PRESTO.

NOW, MY DANIEL!

STEAL AS MUCH POPCORN AS YOU CAN!

MADAM PRESTO

HA HA HA HA HA HA HA

RAD THAI

LATER...

AND NOW...THE STORY OF **MADAME PRESTO**... THE NINETEENTH CENTURY'S MOST **ENIGMATIC** AND **ALLURING** MAGICIAN!

IT WAS SAID SHE COULD TURN **INVISIBLE**. **LEVITATE**. **READ MINDS!** THE CLAIMS WERE **ABSURD**, AND YET...AND YET...

YOU STOLE THE **FILM?** I THOUGHT YOU WERE GOING TO STEAL THE **EMERALD!**

FAHH! WHY WOULD I **DO** SUCH A THING?

WE ARE TOGETHER WITH FRIENDS, EATING CANDY BARS AND POPCORN, AND WATCHING **RARE** FOOTAGE OF A MOST INTERESTING WOMAN.

WHAT COULD BE **BETTER?** SOME FOOLISH **EMERALD?**

NO, DANIEL...

...I HAVE STOLEN SOMETHING OF **FAR** GREATER VALUE.

TWELVE HOURS LATER.

THAT FILM WAS MORE IMPORTANT THAN YOU COULD POSSIBLY CONCEIVE.

BOSS...WE THOUGHT THE EMERALD WAS--

CHOOSE A CARD. NOW.

GRAB!

UHH. OH. IT'S ONE OF THE...

...BLACK CARDS.

SSSSSSS

COUGH CHOKE COUGH

GACK!

THE NEXT NIGHT.

YÉ YÉ YÉ!

OH! YÉ YÉ!

OH?

THUCK

OOOOO...

LATER...

BONSOIR, MONSIEUR BRADEN.

AND GOOD EVENING TO *YOU*, BOXLEY.

RUFF!

EVENING, BOXLEY!

WHO'S A GOOD BOY, BOXLEY?

RUFF.

THUCK

RRR?

THUCK

21

LATER STILL...

THUCK

HMPFF. LOAD HER IN THE VAN.

I AM SORRY FOR THE BLINDFOLD.

BUT I COULD NOT HAVE YOU KNOW THE LOCATION OF MY SEVENTH-MOST-SECRET HIDEOUT.

THEN WHY WASN'T *LT. PRICE* BLINDFOLDED?

HELOISE? HAVE YOU MADE A *JOKE?* SHE IS A WOMAN, NO? SHE WOULD NEVER BETRAY A TRUST.

ALTHOUGH IT *IS* TRUE THAT SHE HAS HELPED ME STEAL YOUR *CIGARETTES,* FOR WE WILL HAVE NO SMOKING DURING THIS EVENING'S PROGRAM.

NOW, I BELIEVE YOU KNOW THE OTHERS.

THIS IS *MONSIEUR.* A MASTER CRIMINAL WHOM THE POLICE WOULD *DEARLY* LOVE TO CAPTURE.

HELLO.

&#*%!!!

AND MARGOT, WHO IS *BEAUTIFUL,* AND POSITIONED JUST SO, IN ORDER TO DISTRACT YOU FROM THE PREVIOUS MASTER CRIMINAL.

BONSOIR.

OH.

THIS IS MATADORI. A MASTER OF THE SWORD. BUT SHE IS IN *DISGUISE* SO THAT YOU WILL NOT KNOW HER.

YOU WILL PLEASE *FORGET* THAT IN MY ENTHUSIASM I HAVE MENTIONED HER *NAME.*

PIMENTO!

YIP!

PIETRO!

OINK!

&#%&@!!!

CANDY BARS!

OOH!

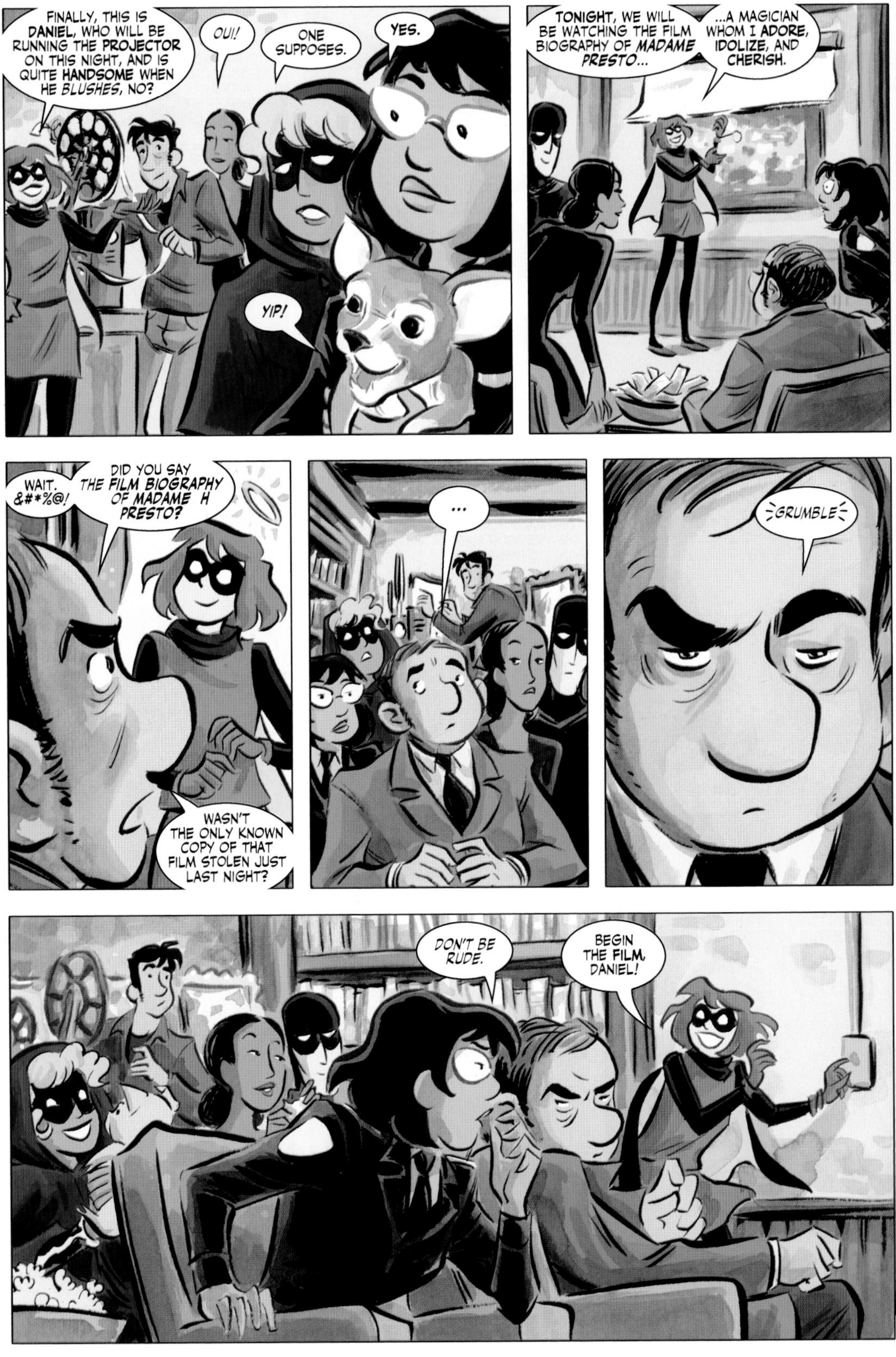
FINALLY, THIS IS DANIEL, WHO WILL BE RUNNING THE PROJECTOR ON THIS NIGHT, AND IS QUITE HANDSOME WHEN HE BLUSHES, NO?
OUI!
ONE SUPPOSES.
YES.
YIP!
TONIGHT, WE WILL BE WATCHING THE FILM BIOGRAPHY OF MADAME PRESTO...
...A MAGICIAN WHOM I ADORE, IDOLIZE, AND CHERISH.
WAIT. &#*%@!
DID YOU SAY THE FILM BIOGRAPHY OF MADAME H PRESTO?
WASN'T THE ONLY KNOWN COPY OF THAT FILM STOLEN JUST LAST NIGHT?
...
GRUMBLE
DON'T BE RUDE.
BEGIN THE FILM, DANIEL!

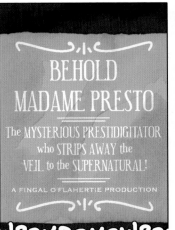

BEHOLD
MADAME PRESTO
The MYSTERIOUS PRESTIDIGITATOR
who STRIPS AWAY the
VEIL to the SUPERNATURAL!

A FINGAL O'FLAHERTIE PRODUCTION

WRRKRRKRWRR

KRRKRWRRKRR

THERE'S NO SOUND?

House lights DIM as
MADAME PRESTO
begins her DANCE of
SEVEN VICES!

SHUSH, INSPECTOR BELGIQUE. SILENCE IS THE FRIEND OF ALL THIEVES!

RRKRRKRWRRKR

YIP YIP YIP!

GREEN DEMONS
take the stage...

But they are
NO MATCH for the MAGICS of
MADAME PRESTO!

WRRKRRKRWRR

RR.KUNK·KK·RRI

THE FILM IS SOMEWHAT AGED, AND IT SKIPS HERE AND THERE.

DISTRACTING, NO?

SOON...

THANK YOU FOR A LOVELY EVENING. MADAME PRESTO WAS FASCINATING!

SMEK!

MATADORI DEPARTS!

GROINK!

DID YOU NOTICE?

NO, I DON'T THINK SO.

WAS THERE SOMETHING I WAS SUPPOSED TO NOTICE?

YOU HAVE THAT HUNTER'S LOOK IN YOUR EYE.

WHAT DO YOU KNOW OF THE HOUSE OF THE GREEN MASK?

THAT LEGEND? IT'S A MYTH AMONG THIEVES.

"IT CLAIMS THERE WAS A WOMAN WHO MODELED FOR NEARLY ALL OF THE IMPRESSIONIST PAINTERS."

"MANET. RENOIR. TOULOUSE-LAUTREC. PISSARRO. DERAIN. GAUGUIN. VAN GOGH. EVEN VALADON AND DEGAS...

"...THEY ALL COMPLETED PAINTINGS INSPIRED BY A MYSTERIOUS WOMAN.

"A WOMAN WHO TRADED THESE PAINTERS KISSES FOR THEIR ART.

"IT IS SAID SHE WAS KNOWN BY KINGS OF GREAT IMPORT, AND BY THIEVES OF EVEN GREATER IMPORT.

"SHE AMASSED ARTISTIC TREASURES BEYOND COMPARE, GIFTS FROM PAINTERS, MONARCHS, PRINCES, THIEVES, COURTESANS, MUSICIANS, AND SCHOLARS.

"EVERYONE LAID RICHES AT HER FEET."

AND SHE PUT THEM IN A *TREASURE ROOM* IN THE *HOUSE OF THE GREEN MASK.*

BUT DON'T TELL ME *YOU* BELIEVE IN FAIRY TALES?

THE HOUSE HAS BEEN HUNTED FOR OVER A CENTURY. EVEN THE WOMAN'S IDENTITY IS A MYSTERY.

IF THE HOUSE EXISTED, IF THE *WOMAN* EXISTED, THEY WOULD HAVE *LONG* SINCE BEEN DISCOVERED.

YOU MAY AS WELL BE SEARCHING FOR THE *EASTER BUNNY,* OR PURCHASING A TICKET TO RIDE IN *SANTA'S* SLEIGH, OR--

THE FILM SKIPS AFTER THE WORDS *BEHOLD...* THE...HOUSE...OF... THE...GREEN...MASK... TREASURE...AWAITS... WITHIN.

ROWR?

WHAT?

THE FILM. THE WORDS DISPLAYED EACH TIME JUST BEFORE THE FILM SKIPPED.

BEHOLD, THE HOUSE OF THE GREEN MASK. TREASURE AWAITS WITHIN. I'M SURE OF IT.

BUT...CAN THIS BE *TRUE?* DO YOU THINK BANDETTE *KNOWS?*

I THINK SHE *TOLD* ME, IN HER OWN WAY.

BUT...FOR WHAT PURPOSE?

EXCUSE ME, MARGOT?

YES, LT. PRICE?

BANDETTE TOLD US THAT YOU'VE HAD DEALINGS WITH... *THE VOICE?*

OH. YES. THAT MAN.

HE KIDNAPPED MY PARENTS. STOLE MY LIFE. FORCED ME TO INFILTRATE ABSINTHE'S INNER CIRCLE.

STILL... I KNOW LITTLE ABOUT HIM.

I KNOW HIS SPHERE OF INFLUENCE IS IMMENSE, STRETCHING *FAR* ACROSS INTERNATIONAL BOUNDARIES.

I KNOW HE PLAYS WITH LIVES, COLLECTS AND DISCARDS PEOPLE AS IF THEY WERE DOLLS.

I KNOW THERE IS LITTLE CRIME THAT HIS FINGERS HAVE NOT, SOMEHOW, TOUCHED.

I KNOW, TOO, THAT HE WAS ONCE ABSINTHE'S MENTOR...BUT THERE WAS A FALLING-OUT. THEY DESPISE EACH OTHER NOW.

THESE ARE THE THINGS THAT I KNOW.

BUT WHAT I DO *NOT* KNOW IS WHO HE IS.

OR **WHERE** HE CAN BE FOUND.

OR EVEN WHAT HE **LOOKS** LIKE.

...

I FOUND THIS IN ONE OF ABSINTHE'S SAFES.

OH.

YES.

HIS CARDS.

"THE VOICE FORCES VICTIMS TO CHOOSE THEIR OWN FATES. A BLACK CARD IS **DEATH.**

"OTHER CARDS ARE...OTHER THINGS."

$*&@#!!!

I'D ALWAYS THOUGHT **THE VOICE** WAS A *MYTH,* BUT...CERTAIN PAPERS TAKEN FROM ABSINTHE HINT TOWARD HIS **EXISTENCE.**

I SUPPOSE ONE NEVER KNOWS WHEN A MYTH MIGHT BE PROVEN *TRUE.*

MEANWHILE...

AU REVOIR, DANIEL. MAY YOUR NIGHT BE WELL.

SMEK!

HUH?

I HAD FORGOTTEN TO GIVE YOU A KISS. WHAT A FARCE!

WE WOULD BOTH BE RESTLESS IF THIS MATTER WAS NOT RESOLVED.

MAY YOUR NIGHT BE WELL, DANIEL.

THUCK

UNHHHHH...

KRASHH!

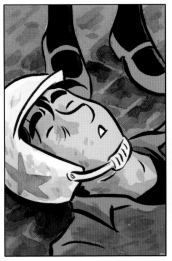

PUT HIM IN THE VAN.

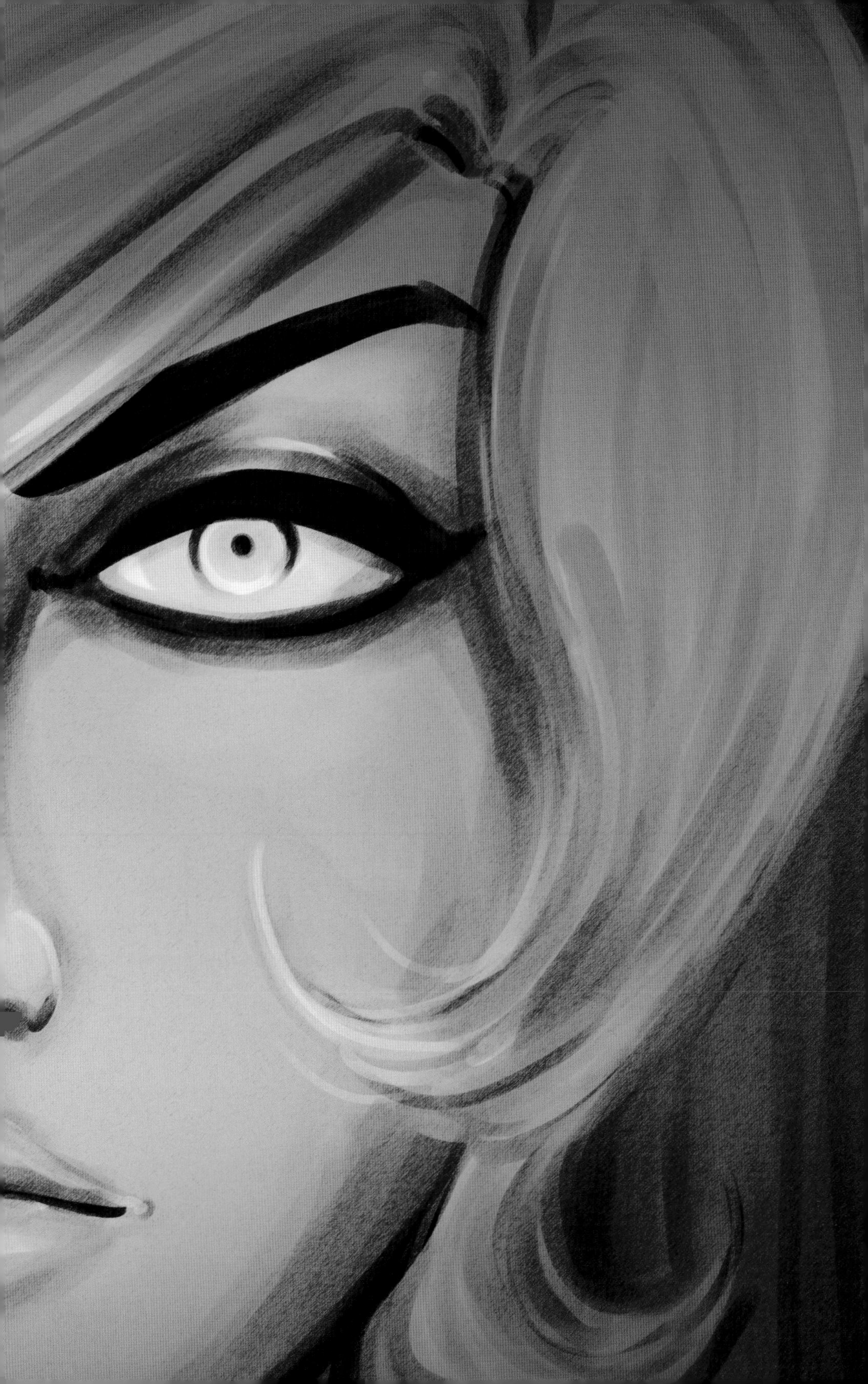

CHAPTER TWO

GRRRR.

I FUME!

PLEASE MAKE SOME ROOM!

I AM FEELING THE NEED TO STOMP!

"DANIEL HAS BEEN KIDNAPPED! TAKEN!"

MAKE SOME MORE ROOM?

YES, PLEASE.

STOMP STOMP STOMP

STOMP STOMP STOMP

35

ADALIND!
KIYOMI!
MANON!
YES, BANDETTE?
PLEASE TALK TO YOUR CONTACTS IN THE CULTURAL ELITE.

WE WILL FLIRT OUTRAGEOUSLY!
OUR EYES WILL WINK!
TONGUES WILL TALK!

FRECKLES!
DALTON!
YOU MUST CALL UPON ALL *DELIVERY DRIVERS*, AND INFORM THEM THAT ONE OF THEIR *OWN* IS MISSING.

"THEIR TYPE HAVE EYES EVERYWHERE, UNRAVELING ALL SECRETS!

STAIR →
ICE ←

105

PIZZA

"IF WORD OF DANIEL CAN BE FOUND, IT IS *DELIVERY MEN* WHO MAY OPEN THE DOORS TO HIS *RESCUE*."

Thank you!

YOU MUST PAY *CAREFUL ATTENTION*, PIMENTO.
BANDETTE IS STILL *STOMPING!*

BRINNGG BRINGG

BRINNGG BRINGG

'ALLO?

SPECIAL POLICE DIVISION. LT. PRICE SPEAKING.

HELOISE! IT IS *I*!

BANDETTE!

THE MASTER THIEF!

CLAP CLAP CLAP

I HAVE CALLED TO LET YOU KNOW I AM *STOMPING*!

STOMP STOMP STOMP

THERE. IT IS KNOWN.

CLIKK

AND NOW, BELDA! SIMONE! EVERYONE!

SEEK OUT CANDY BARS! POPCORNS! BRING BACK *ALL* YOU CAN FIND!

WE MUST HAVE SUPPLIES, FOR AN ARMY MOVES UPON ITS *STOMACH*!

ALTHOUGH I WILL *PERHAPS* MOVE UPON DANIEL'S MOTOR SCOOTER UNTIL HE RETURNS, AS THAT WOULD BE MORE EFFICIENT.

TWO HOURS LATER.

VOILÀ.

SMELL, PIMENTO.

SNIFF SNIFF

FIND OUR DANIEL.

YIP YIP YIP!

AND YOU, SMELL?

RAD THAI

NO? BAHH.

THIS IS WHY LIFE GIVES YOU NOTHING BUT CRUMBS.

AND SO...

GATHER, MY FRIENDS. DANIEL NEEDS YOUR NOSES.

"...FIND HIM."

arf arf!

WOOF!

RUFF RRUFF!

BARK!

YAP!

HARROOOOO!!

I APPEAL TO YOU FOR HELP.

SNIFF

ONE HOUR LATER...

HELLO. MY NAME IS *BANDETTE*.

AND I HAVE STOLEN YOUR PAINTING.

YOUR RODIN SCULPTURE.

THIS FIRST EDITION OF *GULLIVER'S TRAVELS*.

I WILL BE HOLDING THIS PERSIAN PLATE UNTIL SUCH A TIME WHEN MY FRIEND DANIEL IS RETURNED.

YOU WILL USE YOUR CONTACTS.

"YOU WILL USE YOUR RICHES.

"YOU WILL USE YOUR SWAY IN THE COMMUNITY.

"YOU WILL USE YOUR VOICE. YOUR EYES. YOUR FINGERS.

"YOU WILL USE EVERY RESOURCE YOU COMMAND.

"AND MY DANIEL WILL BE RETURNED."

GUHHH.

UNNHG.

HE'S AWAKE!

ARE YOU WELL? OOH-LA-LA! YOU HAVE *SO* MANY BRUISES. A GOOD MANY SCRAPES.

WHERE AM I?

A DUNGEON. AN *INTERROGATION ROOM.*

YOU HAVE BEEN DRUGGED. KIDNAPPED.

IT'S ABOMINABLE.

WHO *ARE* YOU PEOPLE? WHO KIDNAPPED ME? *WHY?*

AH. WE SHOULD INDEED INTRODUCE OURSELVES.

I AM *CASSANDRA.* THIRD DAUGHTER OF THE MOON'S FULL EYE.

WHAT?

WE'RE NOT SURE WHAT THAT MEANS, EITHER. SHE WON'T TELL US.

I'M ABAGAIL. I'M A DANCER.

THIS IS **BOXLEY**, AT LEAST ACCORDING TO HIS **COLLAR**. I THINK HE WAS KIDNAPPED, TOO.

HE STILL HAD A **DART** IN HIM WHEN HE WAS BROUGHT IN.

I'M **CHARLES BITTERS**. I DRY-CLEAN CLOTHES.

I DON'T KNOW **WHY** I'M HERE WITH **YOU** PEOPLE. I WANT TO GO **HOME**. I WANT TO GO TO MY **STORE**.

I'LL MISS MY **BUSINESS**! MY **CUSTOMERS** HAVE THEIR **CLAIM TAGS**!

I HAVE A **RESPONSIBILITY** TO BE THERE. I CAN'T BE IN SOME FOOLISH DUNGEON CAUGHT UP IN WHO KNOWS--

HE TALKS A **LOT**. LIKE THAT.

AND HE'S **WELL NAMED**. **BITTERS**, YOU KNOW.

AS TO YOUR **OTHER** QUESTIONS, WE HAVE **NO IDEA** WHO KIDNAPPED US.

BUT THEY KEEP ASKING US ABOUT SOME...**GREEN HOUSES**?

DO YOU KNOW ANYTHING ABOUT GREEN HOUSES?

GREEN HOUSES?

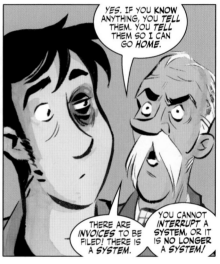

YES. IF YOU **KNOW** ANYTHING, YOU **TELL** THEM. YOU **TELL** THEM SO I CAN GO **HOME**.

THERE ARE **INVOICES** TO BE FILED! THERE IS A **SYSTEM**.

YOU CANNOT **INTERRUPT** A SYSTEM, OR IT IS NO LONGER A **SYSTEM**!

WELL, I MEAN, **GREEN HOUSES** ARE... I SUPPOSE THEY'RE **GREEN**?

WHAT DO YOU KNOW OF **BANDETTE**?

DO YOU MEAN A **SPECIFIC** GREEN HOUSE?

BANDETTE? SHE'S...**UMM**--

SHE'S THAT **CRIMINAL** GIRL. A **BOTHER**! **IMPERTINENT**.

WHY DON'T THE POLICE **DO** SOMETHING ABOUT HER?

...AND NOW WE'RE CAUGHT UP IN SOME **GAME** OF HERS!

I DON'T THINK THAT'S TRUE.

THEY KEEP ASKING ABOUT BANDETTE, BUT THEY DON'T SEEM TO **KNOW** MUCH ABOUT HER.

AND THEY ALSO KEEP ASKING ABOUT SOME WOMAN NAMED **MADAME PRESTO**.

A MAGICIAN? OR A COURTESAN, POSSIBLY?

THEIR OWN STORIES CHANGE.

BUT **WHO'S** ASKING THESE QUESTIONS? WHO ARE--

OH!

THUCK

THUCK

THUCK

RAWRR! RAWRR! RAWRR!

THUCK

RRRRRRR...

UHHH.

DANIEL CAPELLO. MY NAME IS DART PETITE.

YOU WILL COME WITH ME.

ELSEWHERE...

WHEEE!

HA HA HA HA! NOW WE CAN--

OH?

CLICK! CLICK! CLICK!

EHH?

MR. PRIME MINISTER. I HAVE NOW TAKEN THREE PHOTOGRAPHS OF LA INDISCRÉTION.

THEY ARE ARTFULLY FRAMED AND EXQUISITELY LIT, BECAUSE ONE MUST HAVE ART IN ALL THINGS.

THESE PHOTOS WILL BE DESTROYED ONCE MY FRIEND DANIEL HAS BEEN RECOVERED FROM THE CLUTCHES OF A VILLAIN.

YOUR HELP IN THIS MATTER IS APPRECIATED. EVEN, I MUST NOW SAY, DEMANDED.

I COMMEND YOU ON YOUR WHIMSICAL FRIVOLITIES! A PROPER LIFE IS WEIGHTLESS, NO?

THIS IS WHY I REGRET BLACKMAIL. I WOULD STOOP SO LOW FOR NO OTHER BUT MY DANIEL.

PLEASE ACCEPT SEVERAL CANDY BARS AS AN APOLOGY.

FAREWELL.

HMMM.

MUNCH MUNCH

LATER...

SHOULD WE NOT BE HELPING **BANDETTE?** DANIEL HAS GONE MISSING.

I HAVE CERTAIN OF MY **CONTACTS** SEARCHING FOR ANY INFORMATION. IN THE **MEANTIME...**

...AHH, YES, **HERE**...

...WE SEARCH FOR INFORMATION OF **ANOTHER** SORT.

TAP TAP

HELLO?

TAP TAP

OH, YOU HAVE KNOCKED ON MY HEAD.

A **THOUSAND** PARDONS, MADEMOISELLE! I DID NOT THINK THE DOOR WOULD OPEN SO QUICKLY.

AHH, YES, WELL. YOU'RE A **MAN**, AND NOT ALL MEN ARE GOOD AT THINKING.

BUT COME IN, COME IN.

I'LL PUT ON A SPOT OF WHISKEY.

AND SO...

HE WAS A DASHING SORT. DASHED ME OFF TO THE CABARETS.

DASHED OFF MY *STOCKINGS* SOMEWHERE, TOO! I NEVER DID FIND OUT *WHERE!*

BUT, *AHH...* HE WAS A **MAN,** AND A MAN MUST HAVE HIS SECRETS.

HMMM.

NOW WHAT WAS IT YOU WANTED TO TALK TO ME ABOUT AGAIN?

MADEMOISELLE FRANCHESTER, THERE IS A *LETTER* I WISH YOU TO SEE.

"IT WAS RECENTLY DISCOVERED IN A COPY OF A NOVEL BY *RÉTIF DE LA BRETONNE."*

OH, HE WAS A **SCANDALOUS** AUTHOR! THEY CALLED HIM THE **VOLTAIRE OF THE CHAMBERMAIDS!** DID YOU KNOW THAT?

I DID **NOT.** BUT I AM DELIGHTED.

AS YOU CAN **SEE,** THE LETTER, DATED JULY OF **1952,** SPEAKS OF AN OUTRAGEOUS ONGOING AFFAIR.

HMMM. THIS IS **MY** HANDWRITING. IT WAS STEADIER THEN.

"I *KNEW* IT WAS YOUR LETTER, MADEMOISELLE FRANCHESTER. THE *SIGNATURE,* YOU UNDERSTAND. FADED, BUT LEGIBLE. AND AS YOU CAN SEE, THE LETTER LISTS A SERIES OF POSSIBLE MEETING SPOTS."

"MADEMOISELLE FRANCHESTER, IT IS MY BELIEF THAT THESE MEETING PLACES, EACH OF THEM A RESIDENCE, WERE ALL OWNED BY YOUR MYSTERIOUS UNNAMED LOVER. THEY ARE A LIST OF HIS PROPERTIES."

OH?

HA HA HA HA HA!

HERS.

EHH?

HER PROPERTIES. WHY DID YOU ASSUME MY LOVER WAS A MAN?

AHH, YOU MEN WITH YOUR ASSUMPTIONS. IT'S WICKED HOW YOUR THOUGHTS ARE SO BUMPY. DELICIOUS THOUGH. I DO ENJOY YOUR MALE FOOLISHNESS!

YOUR CHINS, TOO. SO STRONG!

OH. THANK YOU, I SUPPOSE.

I'M HAVING MORE WHISKEY. IT'S ONE OF HER BOTTLES, YOU KNOW. AMELIA'S. THE WOMAN I WAS WRITING IN THAT LETTER.

WHY ARE YOU ASKING ME ABOUT HER?

BECAUSE IT IS MY BELIEF THAT THE WOMAN YOU WERE WRITING WAS THE GRANDDAUGHTER OF THE MYSTERIOUS WOMAN KNOWN AS MADAME PRESTO.

...AND I BELIEVE THOSE PROPERTIES IN YOUR LIST HAD ONCE BEEN OWNED BY THE GREAT MAGICIAN HERSELF, GIFTS FROM HER LEGIONS OF ADMIRERS.

OH-HO!

YOU MEN WITH YOUR QUESTS. YOU'RE SO FASCINATING.

I FEEL LIKE A GIRL AGAIN, MONSIEUR CORVID. I FEEL WICKED.

AND NOW I FEEL I UNDERSTAND YOU, TOO.

YOU'RE LOOKING FOR THE HOUSE OF THE GREEN MASK.

ELSEWHERE...

EXCUSE, PLEASE?

I MUST MAKE PROGRESS.

NO? THEN SO BE IT.

IT'S TRUE I AM *MUCH* EXHAUSTED FROM FUMING.

PERHAPS IT IS TIME FOR A SMALL *BREAK,* AND A LARGE CANDY BAR.

UNWRAP UNWRAP UNWRAP

UNWRAP UNWRAP UNWRAP

?

NO, YOU MAY *NOT* HAVE CHOCOLATE.

YOU WERE *MOST* IMPOLITE BY GUARDING THIS SINGLE-LANE BRIDGE WHEN BANDETTE WANTED TO CROSS.

AND SO...

OH?

THUCK

HMMM.

49

YOU.

YES. ME.

DART PETITE!

I BRING WORD FROM... THE VOICE.

IF YOU WOULD LIKE DANIEL TO--

STAY BACK!

IF YOU WANT TO HEAR THIS MESSAGE, THEN YOU--

AHH!

NO!

STAY BACK!

PHOOT!

SPAKK

OH?

THUCK

50

HMMM. YOU ARE UNCONSCIOUS, NO?

THIS ENDS OUR DISCUSSION, THEN.

BUT IF WHAT I HAVE HEARD OF *THE VOICE* IS TRUE, HE WILL HAVE LEFT...

RUSTLE SEARCH RUSTLE

VOILÀ! A RECORDED MESSAGE.

CLIKK

BANDETTE. MEET ME AT THE VICAR'S STAGE. TONIGHT. THREE O'CLOCK. *ALONE.*

OH, ENIGMA AND MYSTERIES!

OUR BREATHLESS HEROINE MUST VENTURE FORTH *ALONE*, BRINGING ONLY HER BRAZEN COURAGE AND A SLIGHTLY INJURED CANDY BAR!

SHE DEPARTS!

OH?

YOUR *PARDON*, MADEMOISELLE FEATHERS.

YOU ARE INTERFERING WITH THE DRAMA.

ADIEU!

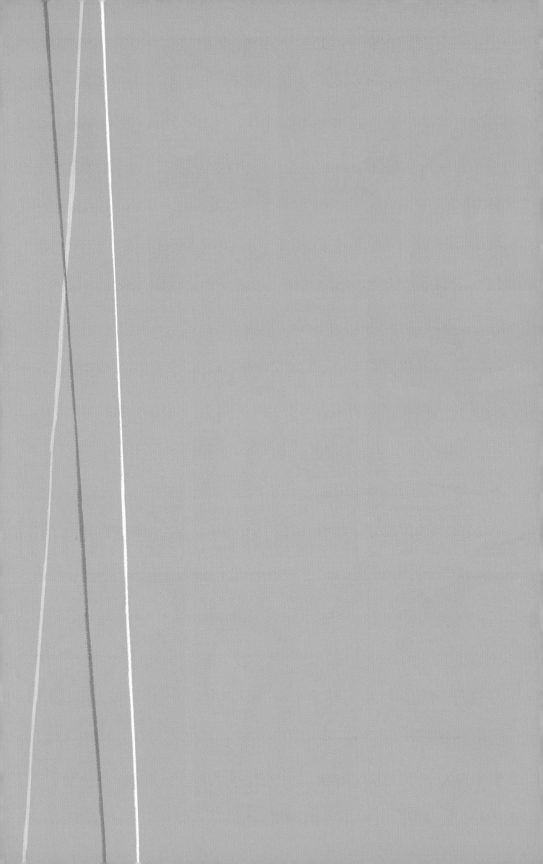

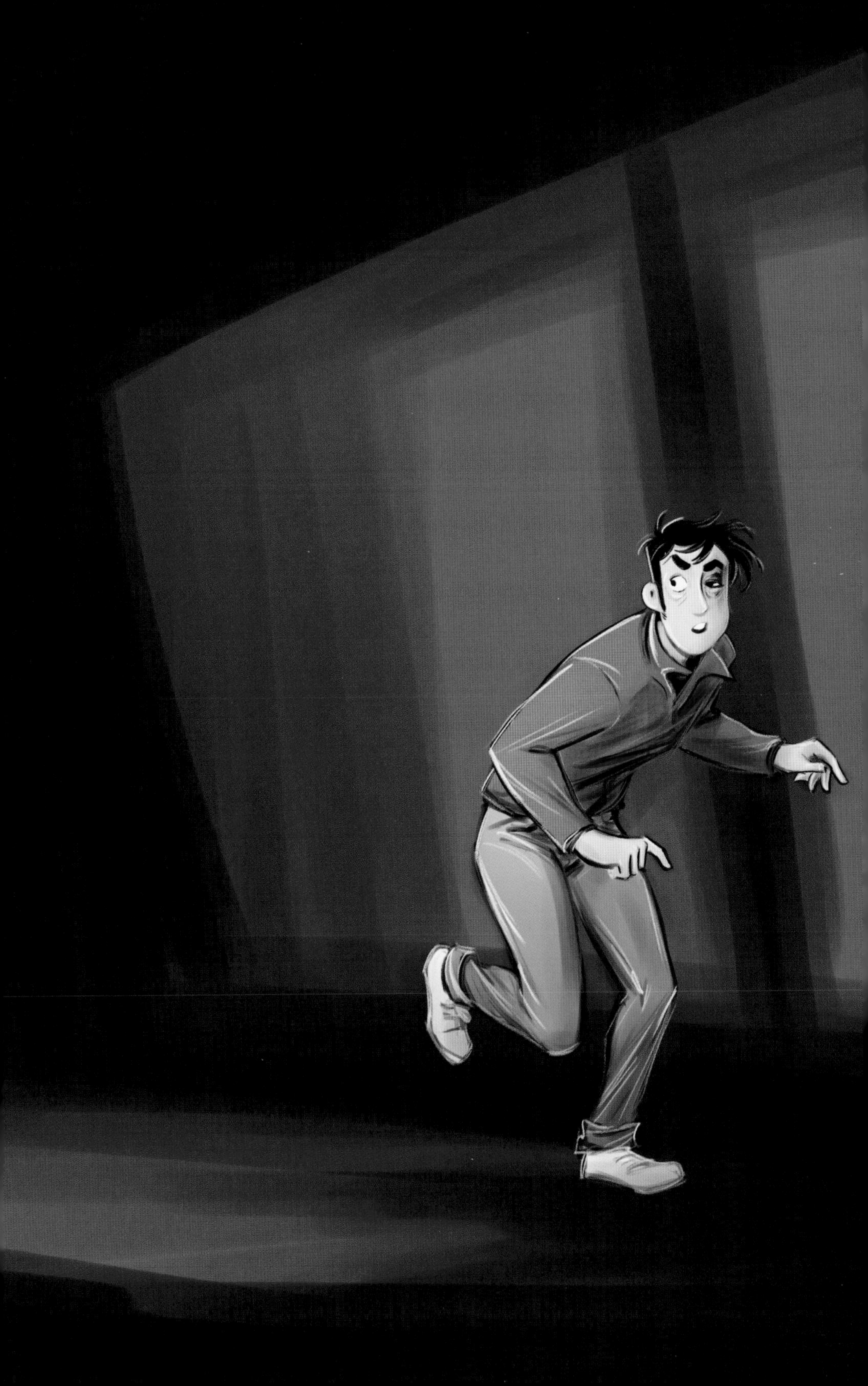

CHAPTER THREE

3 A.M. THE VICAR'S STAGE.

PRESTO!

BANDETTE HAS *ARRIVED!*

HELLO?

BONJOUR ET BONSOIR?

ARE YOU *HERE,* MYSTERIOUS PERSON KNOWN AS *THE VOICE?*

WE ARE TO *MEET,* NO?

I HAVE BROUGHT THIS PILLOW, FOR IT IS QUITE LATE AT NIGHT.

IF YOU ARE *TARDY,* BANDETTE MAY POSSIBLY REQUIRE A NAP.

OH? A *CANDY BAR?*

BIGY CHOCKY

THIS IS A *TRAP,* ONE ASSUMES.

BUT IT IS *ALSO A CANDY BAR,* AND SO ALLOWANCES MUST BE MADE.

CLiKK

HMM, A SPOTLIGHT?

CLIKK

?

AHH, BANDETTE UNDERSTANDS. YOU WISH TO PRESERVE YOUR IDENTITY.

THIS IS WISE, BECAUSE BANDETTE IS **CROSS** WITH YOU. **VERY** CROSS.

YOU HAVE MY **DANIEL,** CORRECT? THIS WILL PROVE TO BE YOUR UNDOING.

NOW, YOUR **PARDON.** I AM HAVING SOMEWHAT OF A PROBLEM FINDING MY **SUNGLASSES.**

IN THE **MEANTIME,** YOU WILL TELL ME WHAT YOU **WANT.**

OUR DISCUSSION HAS ENTERED THE NEGOTIATION STAGE.

I DEMAND THE SAFE RETURN OF MY **DANIEL,** AND...**YOU?**

THE HOUSE OF THE GREEN MASK.

AHH. IT IS AS I PREDICTED.

PERHAPS I SHOULD BE AN **ORACLE.**

YOU WILL **PARDON** THESE CANDY BARS.

I AM STILL HAVING DIFFICULTY FINDING MY **SUNGLASSES.**

IF YOU DO *NOT* PROVIDE ME WITH THE INFORMATION NEEDED TO FIND *THE HOUSE OF THE GREEN MASK,* YOUR *DANIEL* WILL--

AH-HAH!

MY *SUNGLASSES!*

NOW, WHAT WERE WE *SPEAKING* OF? I WAS DISTRACTED BY THE *CANDY BARS* AND HAVE *FORGOTTEN.*

BUT, *WAIT!* DO NOT TELL ME! I WILL MAKE A GUESS.

"WERE WE TALKING OF *ABAGAIL SOVE,* THE KIDNAPPED DANCER WHO IS THE GREAT-GRANDDAUGHTER OF *CARLISSA MOUNTEBANK,* THE GRANDE DAME WHO ONCE OWNED THE *TWICE-SPILLED CABARET?*

OH! YÉ YÉ!

"OR WERE WE TALKING OF *CHARLES BITTERS,* WHO HAS LIKEWISE GONE MISSING? *CHARLES,* AS YOU PERHAPS KNOW, OWNS A STRING OF *WAREHOUSES* ALONG WHAT WAS ONCE KNOWN AS *BURLESQUE ROW,* WHICH ARE RUMORED TO CONTAIN SECRET *ROOMS,* HIDDEN *TUNNELS,* LOST *TREASURES.*"

HOW DO YOU KNOW ABOUT--

AHH. MORE SUNGLASSES!

YOU WILL **HOLD** THESE, YES?

...AND I WILL TELL YOU ABOUT A DOG. NAMED BOXLEY. HE LOOKS LIKE THIS.

YOU WILL UNDERSTAND THAT THIS IS AN APPROXIMATION.

"**BOXLEY** HAS A **KEY** IN HIS COLLAR. DID YOU **KNOW** THAT? HIS OWNER WILL NOT REVEAL WHAT **DOOR** THIS ENIGMATIC KEY UNLOCKS."

X-RAY!

MYSTERIES ARE *QUITE* FETCHING!

DO YOU NOT **ADORE** THEM?

I HAVE FOUND MORE SUNGLASSES.

WHICH DO YOU PREFER?

AND, MR. THE VOICE, DID YOU KNOW THAT THERE ARE *GUARDIANS* TO THE MYSTERIOUS HOUSE OF THE GREEN MASK?

A SECRET SECT OF WARRIORS, BENT ON PROTECTING THE TREASURES FROM CERTAIN MEN WHO ARE ESPECIALLY GREEDY OR UNFORTUNATELY UNSCRUPULOUS.

YOU WILL **NOTICE** THAT I DID NOT MENTION YOU BY **NAME**, BECAUSE BANDETTE IS THE SOUL OF SUBTLETY.

THE NAME OF THE SECT IS THE DAUGHTERS OF THE MOON'S FULL EYE.

INTERESTINGLY, THE THIRD DAUGHTER HAS RECENTLY BEEN KIDNAPPED. THIS IS ACCORDING TO MY SOURCES.

YOUR SOURCES?

"MY SOURCES, YES. THEY ARE URCHINS.

"THEY ARE THOSE WHO WEAR *BADGES.*

"AND THOSE WHO DO *NOT.*"

?

HOWWRROOWW!! arf! BARK! Bark!

"THEY ARE THOSE WHO KNOW **MANSIONS.**

"AND THOSE WHO KNOW THE **STREETS.**"

59

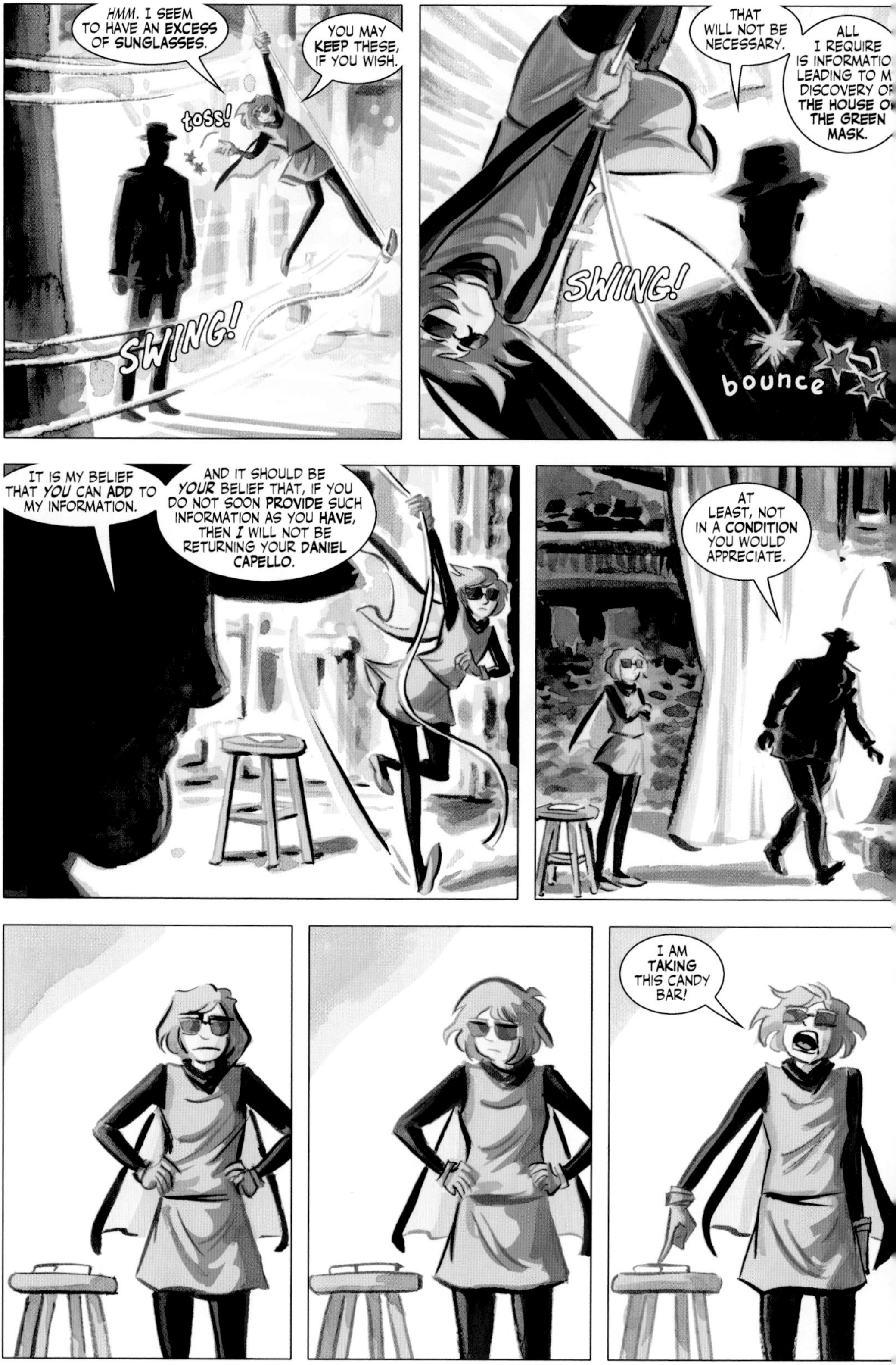

HMM. I SEEM TO HAVE AN EXCESS OF SUNGLASSES.
YOU MAY KEEP THESE, IF YOU WISH.
toss!
SWING!
THAT WILL NOT BE NECESSARY.
ALL I REQUIRE IS INFORMATIO LEADING TO M DISCOVERY OF THE HOUSE O THE GREEN MASK.
SWING!
bounce
IT IS MY BELIEF THAT YOU CAN ADD TO MY INFORMATION.
AND IT SHOULD BE YOUR BELIEF THAT, IF YOU DO NOT SOON PROVIDE SUCH INFORMATION AS YOU HAVE, THEN I WILL NOT BE RETURNING YOUR DANIEL CAPELLO.
AT LEAST, NOT IN A CONDITION YOU WOULD APPRECIATE.
I AM TAKING THIS CANDY BAR!

MEANWHILE...

SHWOOSH!

PERHAPS YOU DON'T KNOW ME.

I AM INSPECTOR B.D. BELGIQUE OF THE SPECIAL POLICE. TODAY, I HAVE *TWO* THINGS.

A LIST OF **MISSING PEOPLE** AND A */@$# SHORTAGE OF PATIENCE.

IT'S TRUE. HE REALLY DOES.

COUGH COUGH

AN HOUR LATER.

CRASH!

KICK!

Ø!Σ$#!

AN HOUR LATER.

9#%®*!!

SKRASH!

BANG!

AN HOUR LATER.

SLAP SLAP SLAP SLAP

@$&Σ#!!!

AN HOUR LATER.

&+@$#%!!!

HE HAS... A **UNIQUE** METHOD OF INVESTIGATION.

SCRUNCH

GAHHH!

HE'S A **UNIQUE** MAN.

AN HOUR LATER.

SSCRREEEEECH!!!

PAFF

SPIFFT

NOW WHAT?

THEY'RE SETTING UP FOR THE PARADE, BELGIQUE.

WE CAN'T GET **THROUGH** UNTIL IT'S OVER.

Ø!*$#!!

£#%®*!!

@$&Σ#!!!

THUMP
THUMP
THUMP

THAP
THAP
THAPP

THUMP

OW.

THERE'S AN **AMUSEMENT PARK** IN TRANSYLVANIA BUILT *UNDERGROUND.* IN AN OLD **SALT MINE.**

YES. THAT TRANSYLVANIA. WITH THE *DRACULAS.*

63

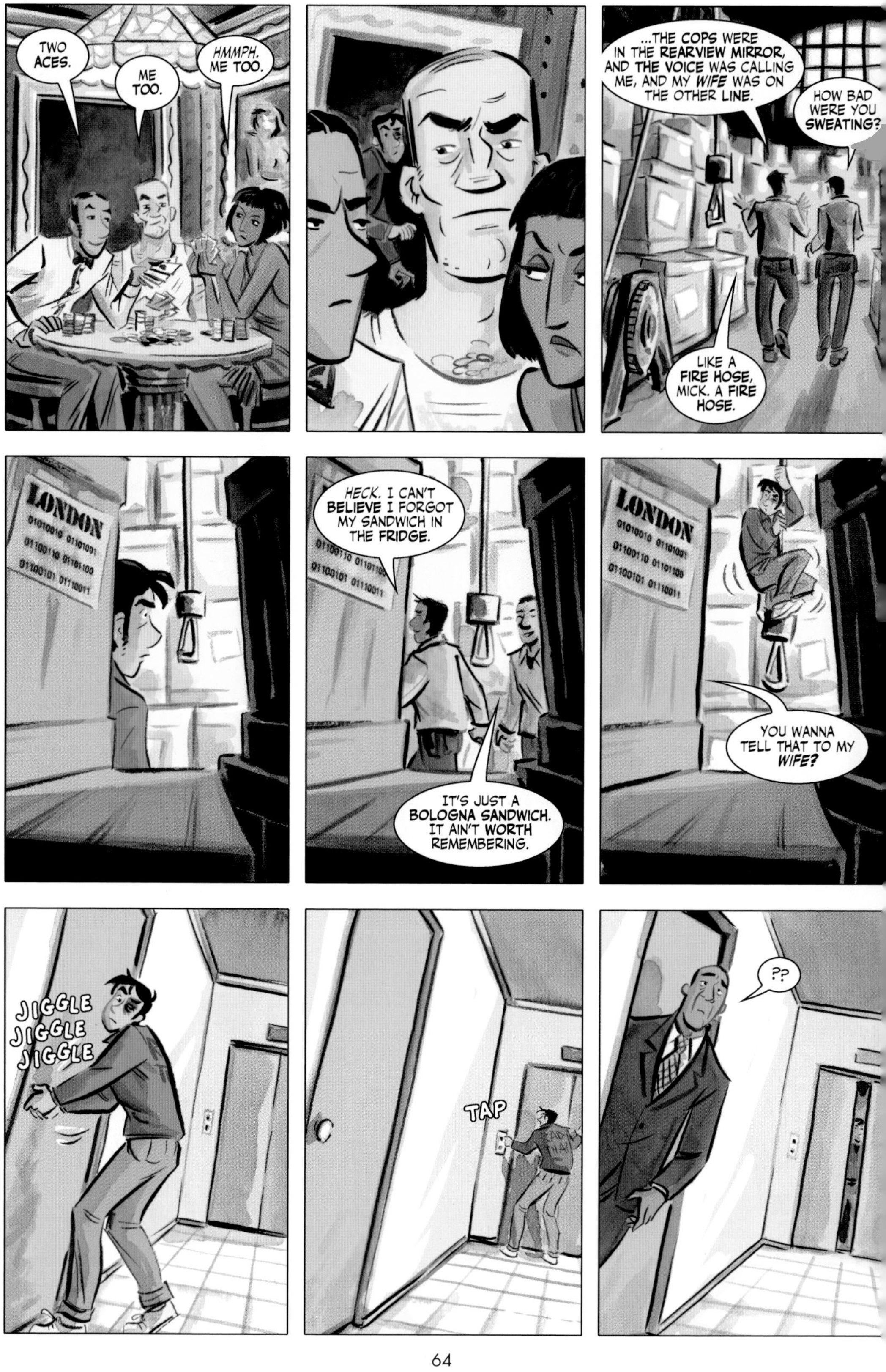
TWO ACES.
ME TOO.
HMMPH. ME TOO.
...THE **COPS** WERE IN THE **REARVIEW MIRROR**, AND **THE VOICE** WAS CALLING ME, AND MY ***WIFE*** WAS ON THE OTHER **LINE**.
HOW BAD WERE YOU **SWEATING?**
LIKE A **FIRE HOSE**, MICK. A **FIRE HOSE**.
LONDON
01010010 01101001
01100110 01101100
01100101 01110011
HECK. I CAN'T **BELIEVE** I FORGOT MY SANDWICH IN THE **FRIDGE**.
IT'S JUST A **BOLOGNA SANDWICH**. IT AIN'T **WORTH** REMEMBERING.
YOU WANNA TELL THAT TO MY ***WIFE?***
JIGGLE JIGGLE JIGGLE
TAP
??

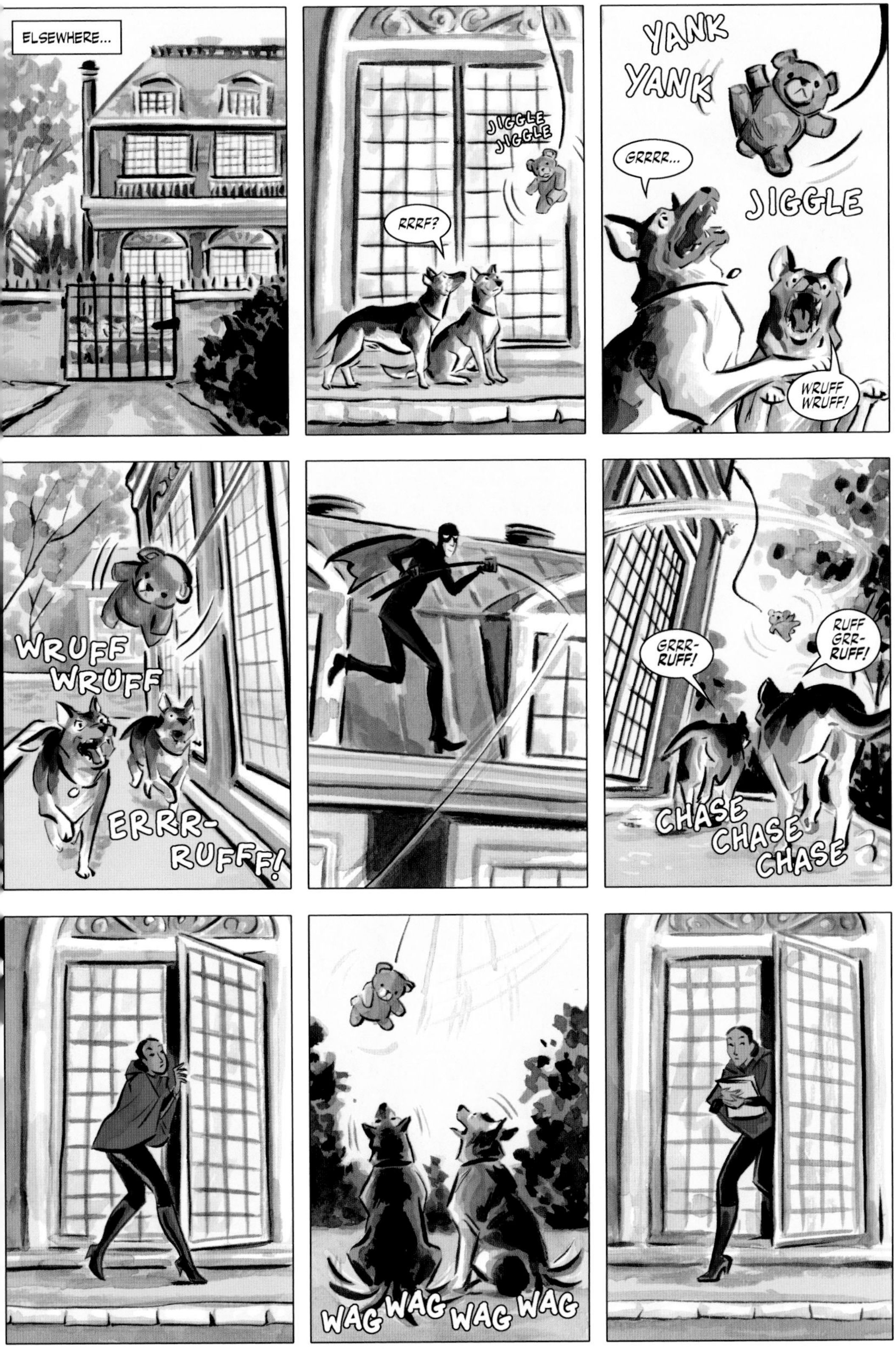
ELSEWHERE...
JIGGLE JIGGLE
RRRF?
YANK
YANK
GRRRR...
JIGGLE
WRUFF WRUFF!
WRUFF
WRUFF
ERRR-
RUFFFF!
GRRR-RUFF!
RUFF GRR-RUFF!
CHASE
CHASE
CHASE
WAG WAG WAG WAG

MEANWHILE...

BONJOUR AND GOOD MORNING AND HELLO, MES URCHINS!

IT IS *I*, BANDETTE, THE KING AND QUEEN OF THIEVES!

IT IS TIME FOR A *REPORT!*

THE VOICE LEFT THE THEATER SHORTLY AFTER THREE LAST NIGHT. I FOLLOWED HIM TO THE HOTEL POMPADOUR...

"...WHERE HE STAYED THE ENTIRE NIGHT, WITH *MYSELF* KEEPING CLOSE WATCH, QUITE VIGILANT!"

SNOOORRE!!!

BUT THE SCURRILOUS ROGUE IS LEAVING NOW. ARE YOU PREPARED TO FOLLOW HIM? ARE YOU IN POSITION?

YES.

YES!

YES.

READY!

OUI!

THIS IS GOOD. NOW, YOU MUST UNDERSTAND THAT *BANDETTE* WILL BE IN DISGUISE!

YOU CANNOT *TELL* THIS OVER THE AIR, BECAUSE MY *VOICE* IS THE SAME, NO?

KEEP IN MIND THAT YOU MAY NOT RECOGNIZE ME IN PERSON, THOUGH, FOR MY DISGUISE IS QUITE CLEVER.

NOW, THE GAME BEGINS! YOU HAVE HIS TRAIL, THEN?

YES!

YES.

YES!

OUI!

BELDA? DO YOU *SEE* HIM?

YES! CAN I KEEP THE BALLOONS?

OUI. YOU MAY *KEEP* THE BALLOONS.

AND THERE WILL ALSO BE *CAKE* WHEN WE RECOVER *DANIEL!*

I WANT CAKE!!!

SHUSH, BELDA. STEALTH IS OUR FRIEND.

AS IS CAKE.

EXCUSE ME.

I AM IN DISGUISE.

EXCUSEZ-MOI. DID YOU PERHAPS SEE A WIDE MAN WITH AN UNFORTUNATE HAT PASS BY?

AND DO NOT WORRY. I AM NOT AN EVIL WITCH. I AM IN DISGUISE.

HE WENT THAT WAY. I THINK HE GOT INTO A BIG BLACK CAR.

DO NOT FEAR, PIGEONS. I AM IN DISGUISE.

I AMEND MY EARLIER STATEMENT.

I AM NOT IN DISGUISE.

YOUR PARDON FOR THE CONFUSION BUT I HAVE NOT HAD MY BREAKFAST AND COULD PERHAPS USE SOME CHOCOLATE.

HE IS IN *SIGHT*, MANON?

YES, BANDETTE. HE IS.

PIMENTO?

ARF!

FRECKLES, YOU WILL PRETEND THAT YOU DO NOT KNOW ME, FOR I AM IN DISGUISE.

ARE YOU...A *MOTH?*

YES. THERE IS A PARADE. I WILL BLEND IN, AS IF I WERE A GHOST.

AND IN THIS CASE, ALSO A *MOTH.*

BUZZZZZ!!

BANDETTE. THIS IS *HELOÏSE.* THE VOICE HAS JUST GONE INTO A WAREHOUSE.

MAYBE THAT'S WHERE THEY'RE HOLDING *DANIEL?*

PLAFF!

MEANWHILE...

THIS IS AN *INCREDIBLE* TREASURE TROVE OF PAPERS, MARGOT. SPANNING DECADES!

I *KNOW!* LOOK, HERE'S A LETTER FROM OSCAR WILDE! AND ANOTHER FROM JANE BOWLES!

AND HERE'S ONE FROM *MADAME PRESTO* HERSELF!

THESE...THESE ARE ALL CORRESPONDENCE BETWEEN **MADAME PRESTO** AND HER FRIENDS AND LOVERS.

SHE SEEMS TO HAVE BEEN A NAUGHTY WOMAN.

I *HEAVILY* SUSPECT I WOULD HAVE LIKED HER.

WE'RE NOT LOOKING FOR RISQUÉ GOSSIP RIGHT NOW, THOUGH.

SEE IF YOU CAN FIND ANY MENTION OF **THE HOUSE OF THE GREEN MASK.** ANY HINT OF A LOCATION. AN ADDRESS.

PASS ME THE BISCUITS, IF YOU WILL. AND THE JAM.

HERE YOU ARE, LEON.

THIS IS ALL SO *AMAZING!* I'VE FOUND A LETTER FROM AMELIA EARHART!

AND HERE'S ONE FROM THE CARTOONIST WINSOR MCCAY. THERE'S EVEN A DRAWING OF MADAME PRESTO WITH LITTLE NEMO. IT'S SO CHARMING!

IT'S TOO BAD WE'RE NOT LOOKING FOR RISQUÉ GOSSIP, BECAUSE **HERE'S** A LETTER TO HENRI MATISSE WITH AN ENCLOSED PICTURE OF MADAME PRESTO AS SHE--

OH!

I THINK I'VE FOUND SOMETHING.

ACROSS THE CITY...

IT WOULD BE **ENTIRELY RECKLESS** TO ATTEMPT ANY ATTACK ON THE ENEMY HEADQUARTERS.

EXCUSE ME, DEAR PIGEONS. I AM BEING FOOLISH.

?

URCHINS! WE HAVE AN **EMERGENCY!**

AT A **WAREHOUSE** THE COLOR OF A CANDY BAR!

CLIK!

DO YOU THINK I SHOULD HAVE **SPECIFIED** WHAT COLOR OF CANDY BAR I MEANT?

THERE ARE **MANY KINDS** OF CANDY BARS, YOU KNOW.

YOU MUST TELL BANDETTE YOUR **OWN** FAVORITES.

ROOF CCESS

NO SMOKING ON ROOF!

NO CARD PLAYING ON ROOF!

IF YOU LIKE **CHOCOLATE,** THERE IS A *CHOCOLATIER* NEXT TO THE PARK I BELIEVE YOU WOULD ENJOY.

BUT, *AH.* YOU ARE A CAT. I WONDER, ARE THERE CATNIP CANDY BARS?

FWAPPP!

OH?

ROOF ACC...

AVERT YOUR EYES, MR. TABBY. I AM GOING TO KISS A BOY.

SMEKK!

NOW THEN, LET US MAKE OUR ESCAPE.

THE CAT AND I WERE DISCUSSING A VISIT TO A CHOCOLATIER. YOU WILL PERHAPS HAVE AN OPINION?

COME, YOU ARE TO BE TREATED AS A PRINCE IN MY SECRET HEADQUARTERS.

ONCE YOU ARE RESTING, I WILL RETURN TO THESE PREMISES, CONFRONT YOUR KIDNAPPERS, AND DISCUSS THIS BLACK EYE OF YOURS.

DANIEL...ARE YOU COMING?

I CAN'T LEAVE WITHOUT THE OTHERS.

ABAGAIL. AND BOXLEY. WE NEED TO RESCUE THEM.

I CAN'T LEAVE WITHOUT--

thwissh!

YOU CANNOT LEAVE AT ALL.

71

DART PETITE!

AH, THE VILLAINESS APPEARS!

THIS MEANS YOU WOULD LIKE TO BE UNCONSCIOUS AGAIN, YES?

NO. WHAT I WANT IS TO *SHOOT* YOU.

AND *THIS* TIME, THERE IS NO KNOCKOUT DRUG. THESE DARTS ARE TIPPED WITH POISON.

QUITE FATAL.

MEANWHILE...

%¡*$#& THIS PARADE!

EHH, WOT? I'M RATHER ENJOYING IT!

AND...

DID YOU ALL GET THE DISTRESS CALL?

YES! HAS SHE FOUND DANIEL?

WE MUST HURRY!

CAKE!

AARF!

BEHIND ME, DANIEL.

MAKE YOUR WAY TO THE WIRE.

YOU MUST *CROSS*.

ERR.

TOO LATE. THE HUNTER HAS FOUND HER PREY.

THE DIE IS CAST, AND...

"...THE DART IS FIRED."

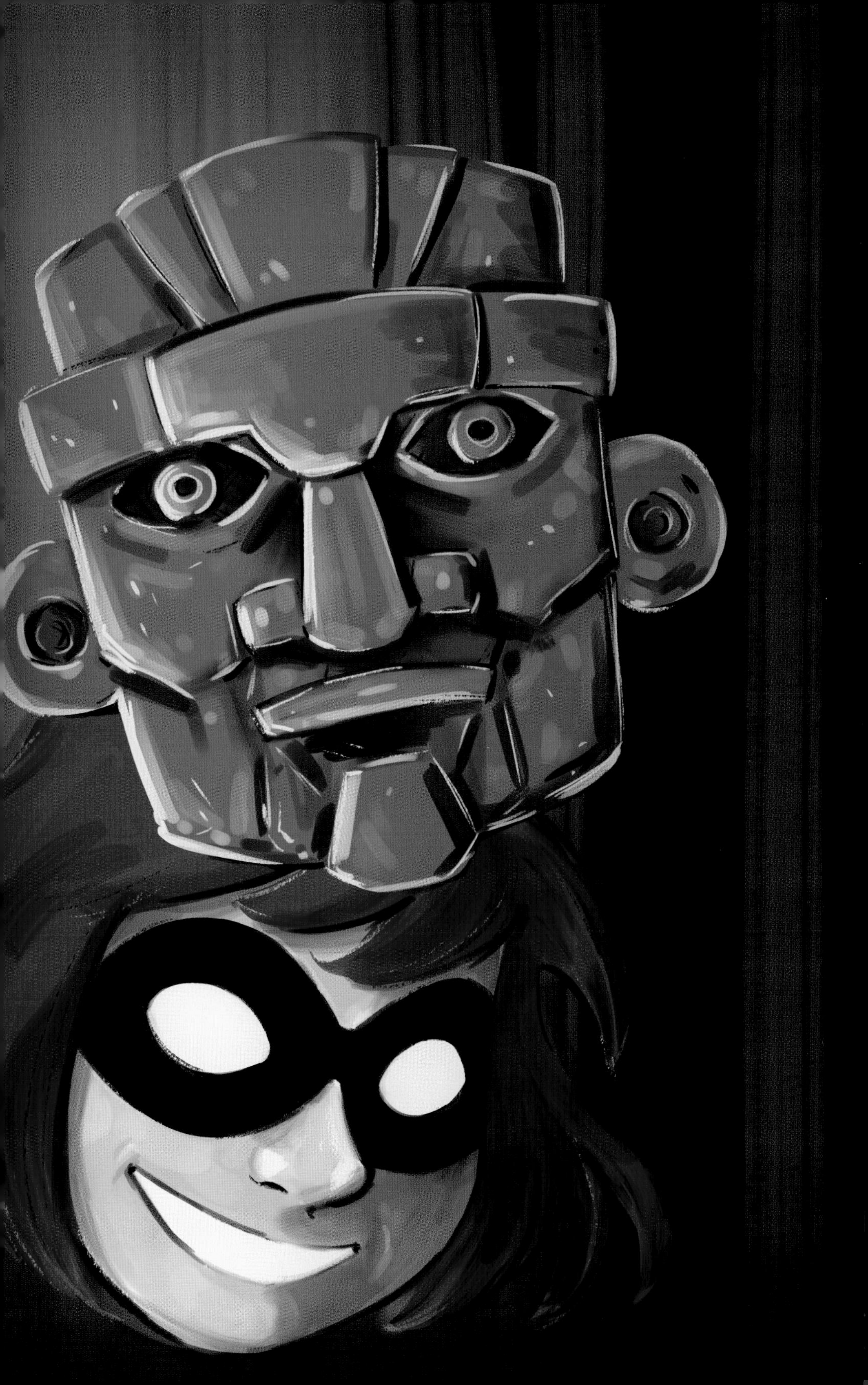

CHAPTER FOUR

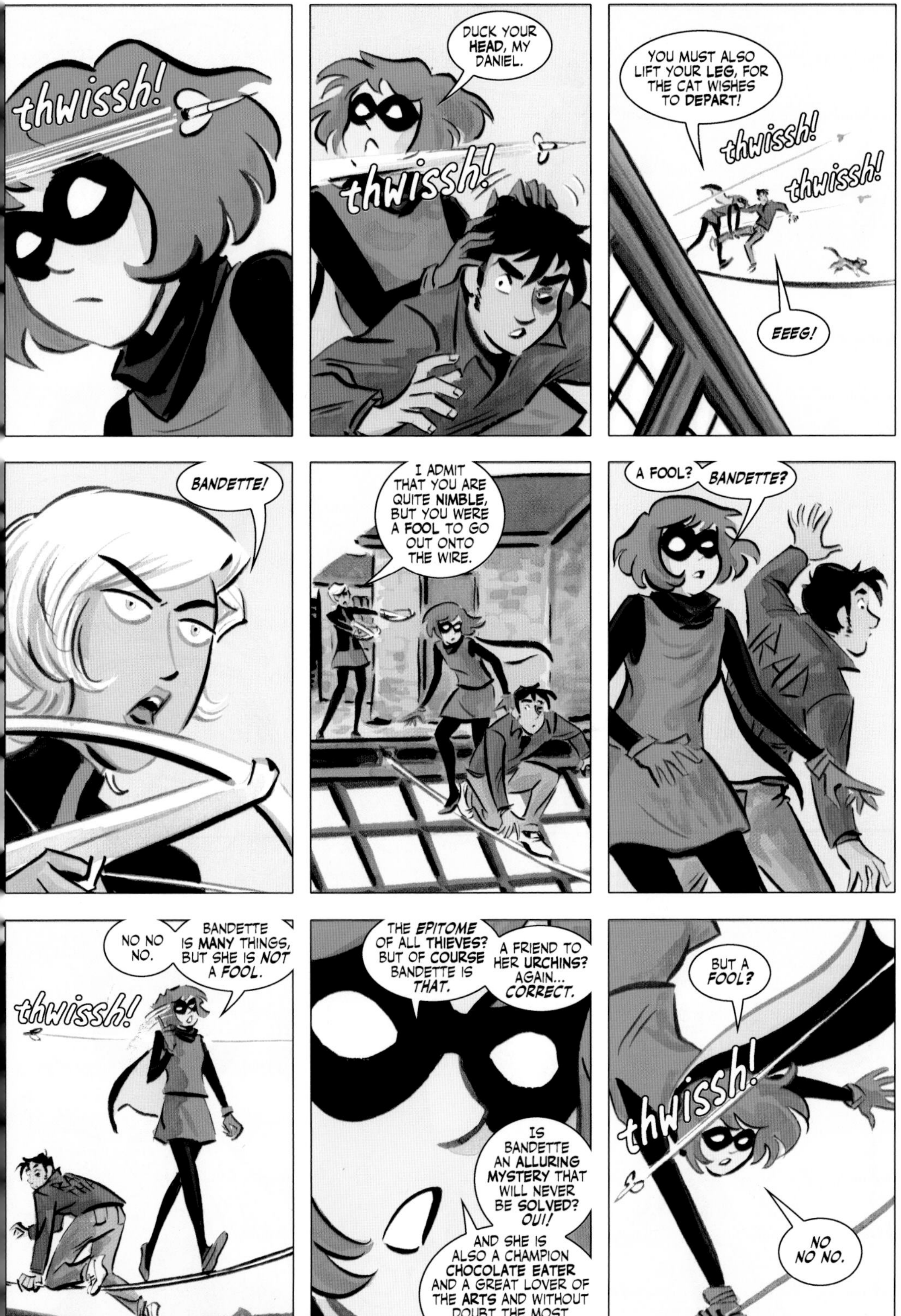
thwissh!
DUCK YOUR HEAD, MY DANIEL.
thwissh!
YOU MUST ALSO LIFT YOUR LEG, FOR THE CAT WISHES TO DEPART!
thwissh!
thwissh!
EEEG!
BANDETTE!
I ADMIT THAT YOU ARE QUITE NIMBLE, BUT YOU WERE A FOOL TO GO OUT ONTO THE WIRE.
A FOOL?
BANDETTE?
NO NO NO.
BANDETTE IS MANY THINGS, BUT SHE IS NOT A FOOL.
thwissh!
THE EPITOME OF ALL THIEVES? BUT OF COURSE BANDETTE IS THAT.
A FRIEND TO HER URCHINS? AGAIN... CORRECT.
IS BANDETTE AN ALLURING MYSTERY THAT WILL NEVER BE SOLVED? OUI!
AND SHE IS ALSO A CHAMPION CHOCOLATE EATER AND A GREAT LOVER OF THE ARTS AND WITHOUT DOUBT THE MOST CHARMING OF ALL FEMMES.
BUT A FOOL?
thwissh!
NO NO NO.

WHAT IS FOOLISH IS TO NEVER DO FOOLISH THINGS!

thwissh!

FOR HOW ELSE DO WE LIVE?

IT IS FAR TOO DEPRESSING TO LIVE IN A BOX.

MUCH BETTER TO LIVE ON THE WIRE!

thwissh!

thwissh!

ON THE EDGE!

thwissh!

ON YOUR HEAD!

B-DONK!

GUFF!

AND NOW, DART PETITE, FEAST YOUR NEFARIOUS EYES ON THIS!

WATCH AND BE ASTOUNDED AS THE WORLD'S GREATEST THIEF MAKES THE WORLD'S GREATEST LEAP, AND...

TUP!

...ATTACKS!

SWOOSH!

76

?.?.?

HAH! YOU MISSED!

OH? DO YOU THINK SO?

WERE YOU NOT PAYING ATTENTION?

I AM THE WORLD'S GREATEST THIEF.

I HAVE STOLEN YOUR POINTY SHOOTER THINGIES.

THEY ARE NOW GARBAGE. MERE REFUSE.

I DISCARD THEM, THUS...

FWOOP

AND NOW, WE ENTER INTO A FAR MORE PLEASANT PORTION OF OUR DISCUSSION.

WE WILL SPEAK OF HOW YOU SHOT AT ME.

STAY BACK! STAY AWAY FROM ME!

AND WE WILL SPEAK OF HOW YOU KIDNAPPED MANY OTHERS.

AND MOST IMPORTANTLY, WE WILL DISCUSS...

HOW YOU HARMED MY DANIEL.

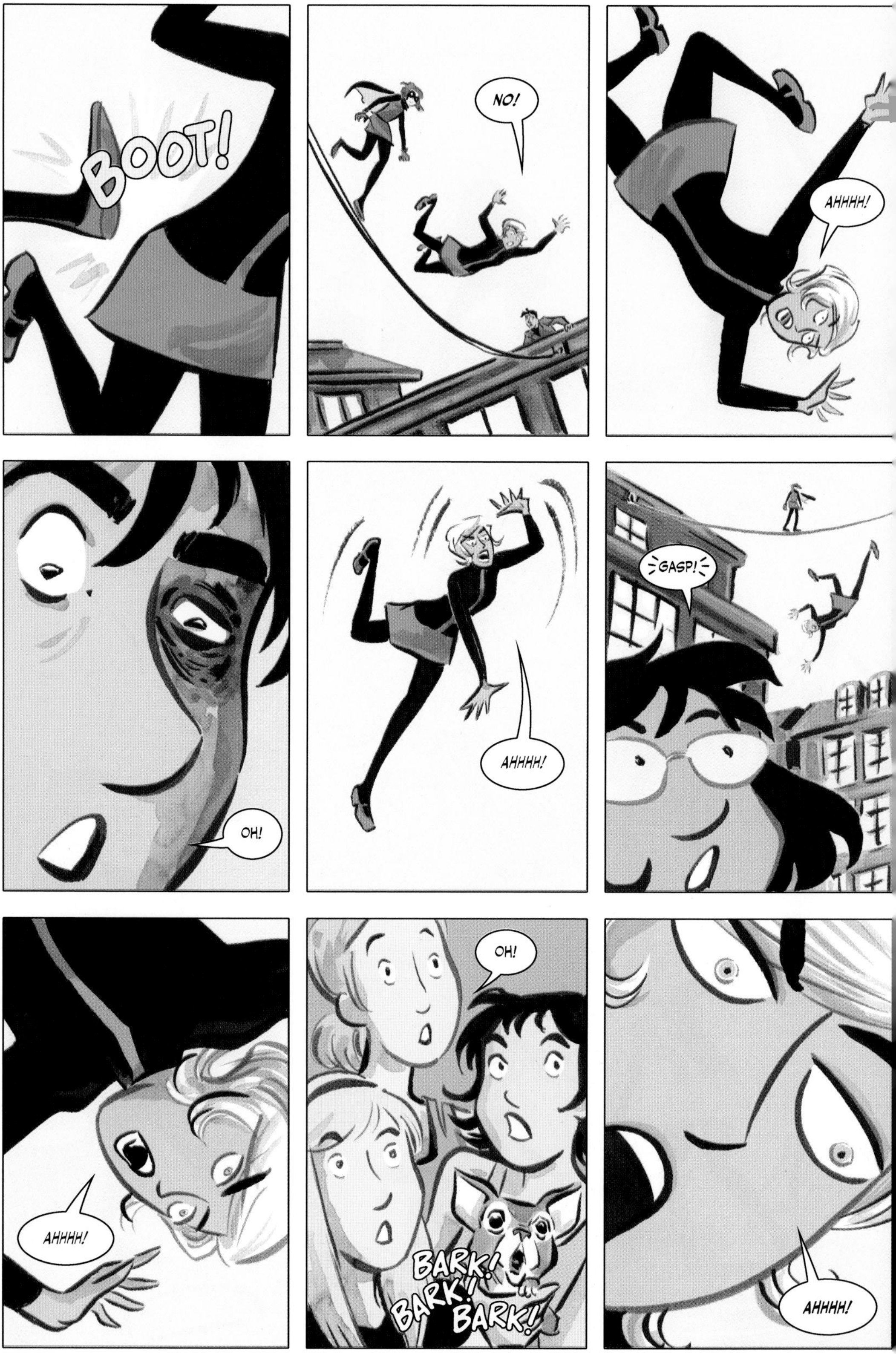
BOOT!
NO!
AHHHH!
OH!
AHHHH!
GASP!
AHHHH!
OH!
BARK! BARK! BARK!
AHHHH!

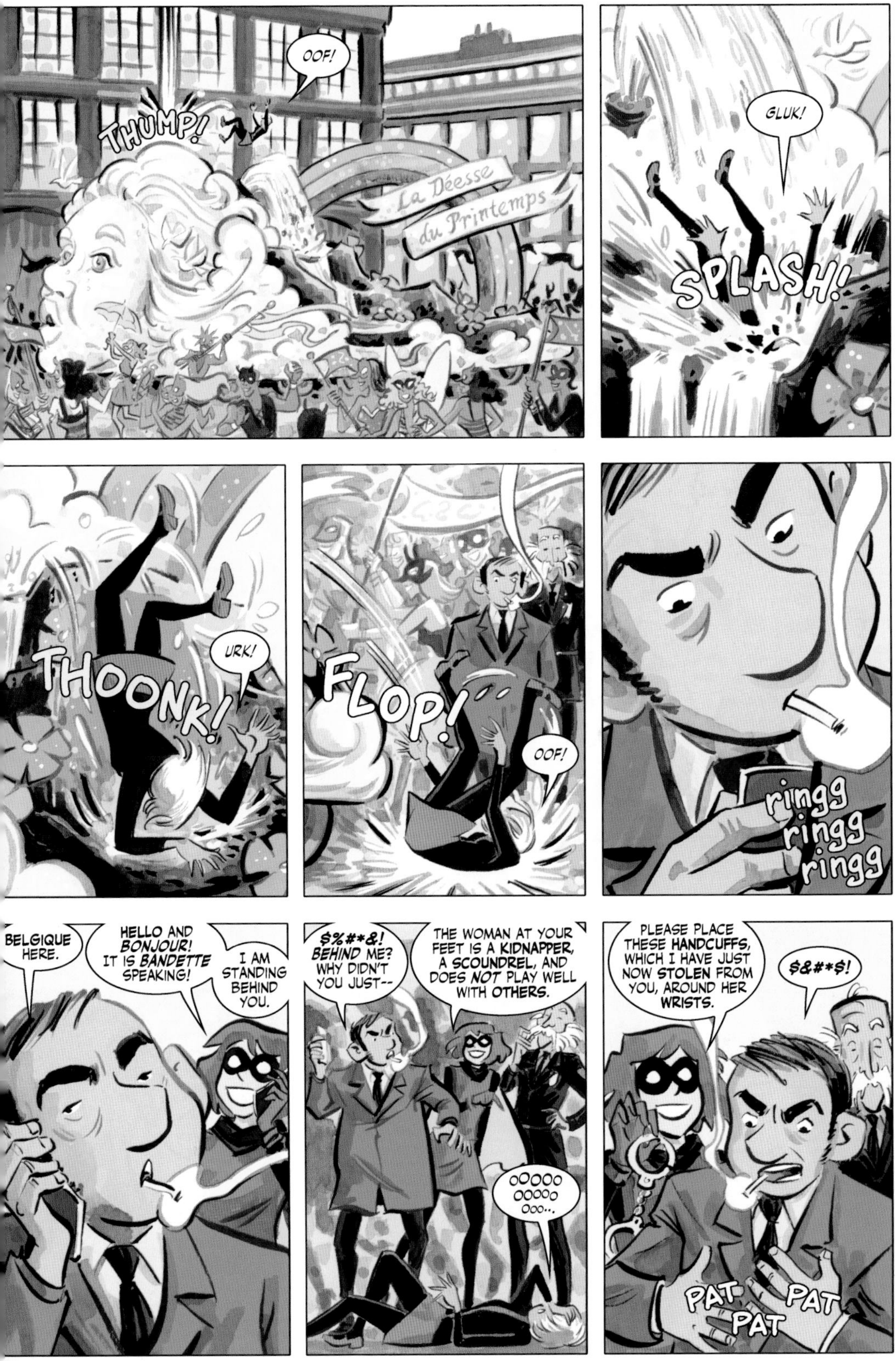
THUMP!
OOF!
La Déesse du Printemps
GLUK!
SPLASH!
THOONK!
URK!
FLOP!
OOF!
ringg ringg ringg
BELGIQUE HERE.
HELLO AND BONJOUR! IT IS BANDETTE SPEAKING!
I AM STANDING BEHIND YOU.
$%#*&! BEHIND ME? WHY DIDN'T YOU JUST--
THE WOMAN AT YOUR FEET IS A KIDNAPPER, A SCOUNDREL, AND DOES NOT PLAY WELL WITH OTHERS.
OOOOO OOOOO OOO...
PLEASE PLACE THESE HANDCUFFS, WHICH I HAVE JUST NOW STOLEN FROM YOU, AROUND HER WRISTS.
$&#*$!
PAT PAT PAT

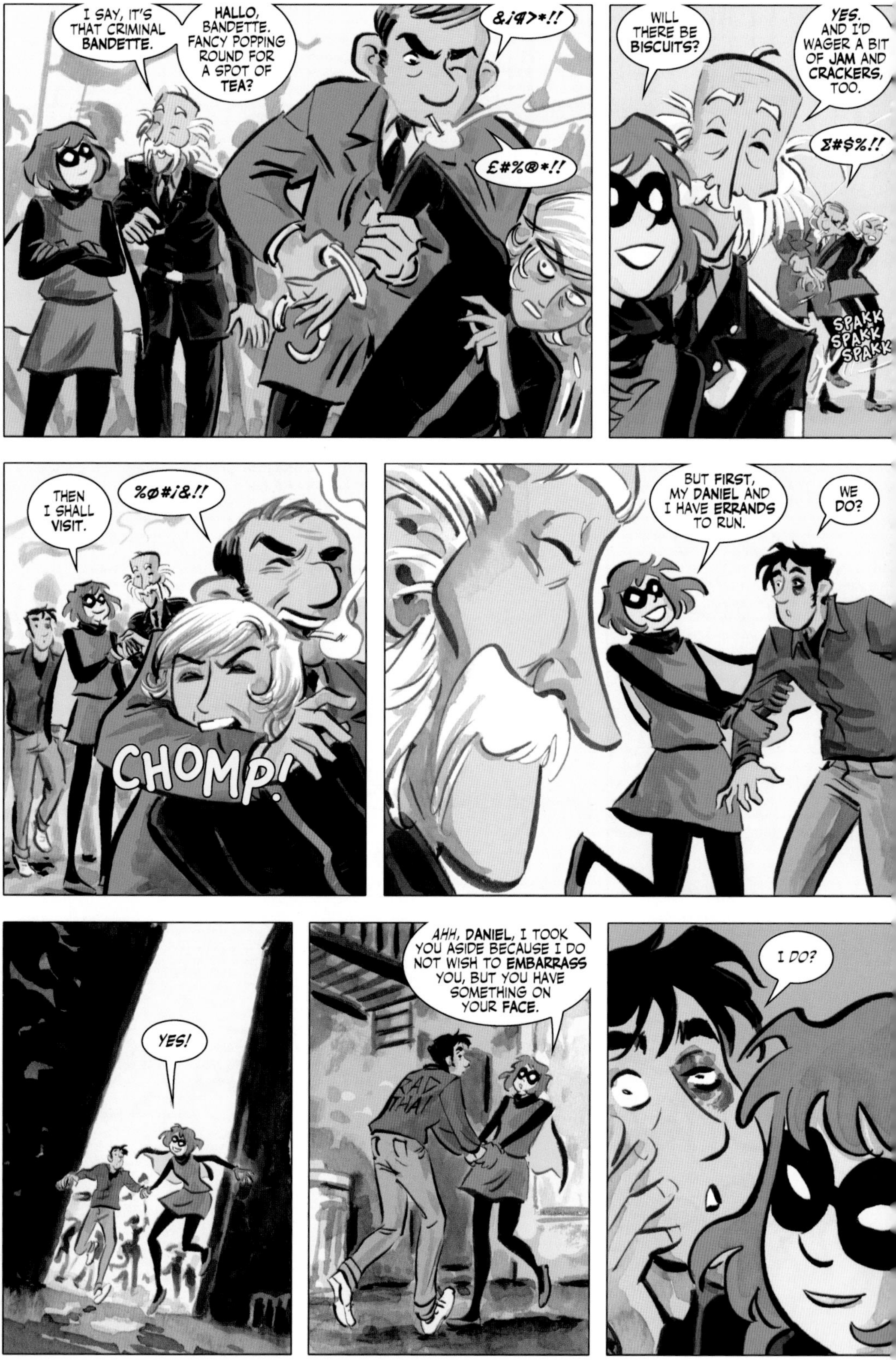
I SAY, IT'S THAT CRIMINAL BANDETTE.
HALLO, BANDETTE. FANCY POPPING ROUND FOR A SPOT OF TEA?
&¡¶>*!!
£#%®*!!
WILL THERE BE BISCUITS?
YES. AND I'D WAGER A BIT OF JAM AND CRACKERS, TOO.
Σ#$%!!
SPAKK SPAKK SPAKK
THEN I SHALL VISIT.
%Ø#¡&!!
CHOMP!
BUT FIRST, MY DANIEL AND I HAVE ERRANDS TO RUN.
WE DO?
YES!
AHH, DANIEL, I TOOK YOU ASIDE BECAUSE I DO NOT WISH TO EMBARRASS YOU, BUT YOU HAVE SOMETHING ON YOUR FACE.
I DO?

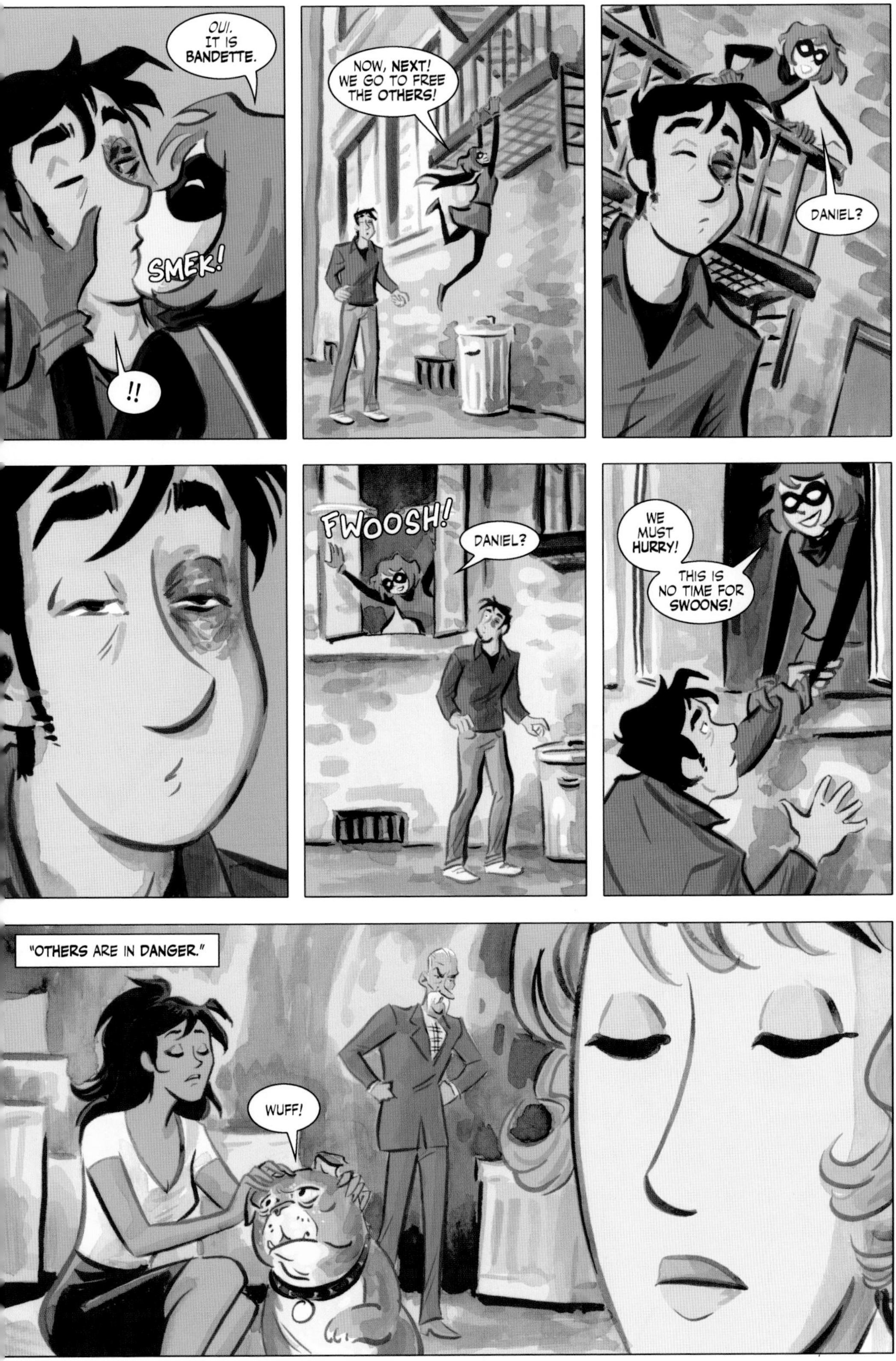

OUI. IT IS BANDETTE.
SMEK!
!!
NOW, NEXT! WE GO TO FREE THE OTHERS!
DANIEL?
FWOOSH!
DANIEL?
WE MUST HURRY!
THIS IS NO TIME FOR SWOONS!
"OTHERS ARE IN DANGER."
WUFF!

BUT THERE ARE SO MANY GUARDS. WE'LL HAVE TO BE CAREFUL.

YES. OF COURSE.

CAUTION IS BANDETTE'S VERY NATURE.

!!

NHHH?

OH?

VOILÀ!

BANG!

BANG!

SPAK!

BANG!

LIKE SO!

PIP!

PING!

BANDETTE ENTERS INTO DEBATE!

AND THIS!

OOF!

THOOP!

AND ALSO... THIS!

MUNCH MUNCH MUNCH

THUMP

GAHH!

AND THIS!

SLIDE!

PLEASE TAKE CARE WITH YOUR PISTOL, MADEMOISELLE FELON!

THEY ARE TRÈS DANGEREUX!

FWOOP!

BANG!

BANG!

WHUMP

DID YOU ALL HEAR THAT?

WHUFF!

BANG! BANG! BANG! BANG! BANG!

OUCH! LOOK OUT!

THUMP!

CLATTER CLATTER

SHE'S OVER THERE!

ABOVE YOU!

BEHIND YOU!

BELOW YOU!

SHE'S ON YOUR LEFT!

NO, YOUR OTHER LEFT!

CRASH!

THUMP!

AAH!

CL!KK

PRESTO!

YOUR PARDON FOR THE CLAMOR.

IT SEEMS I WAS NOT INVITED.

UHNNNN...

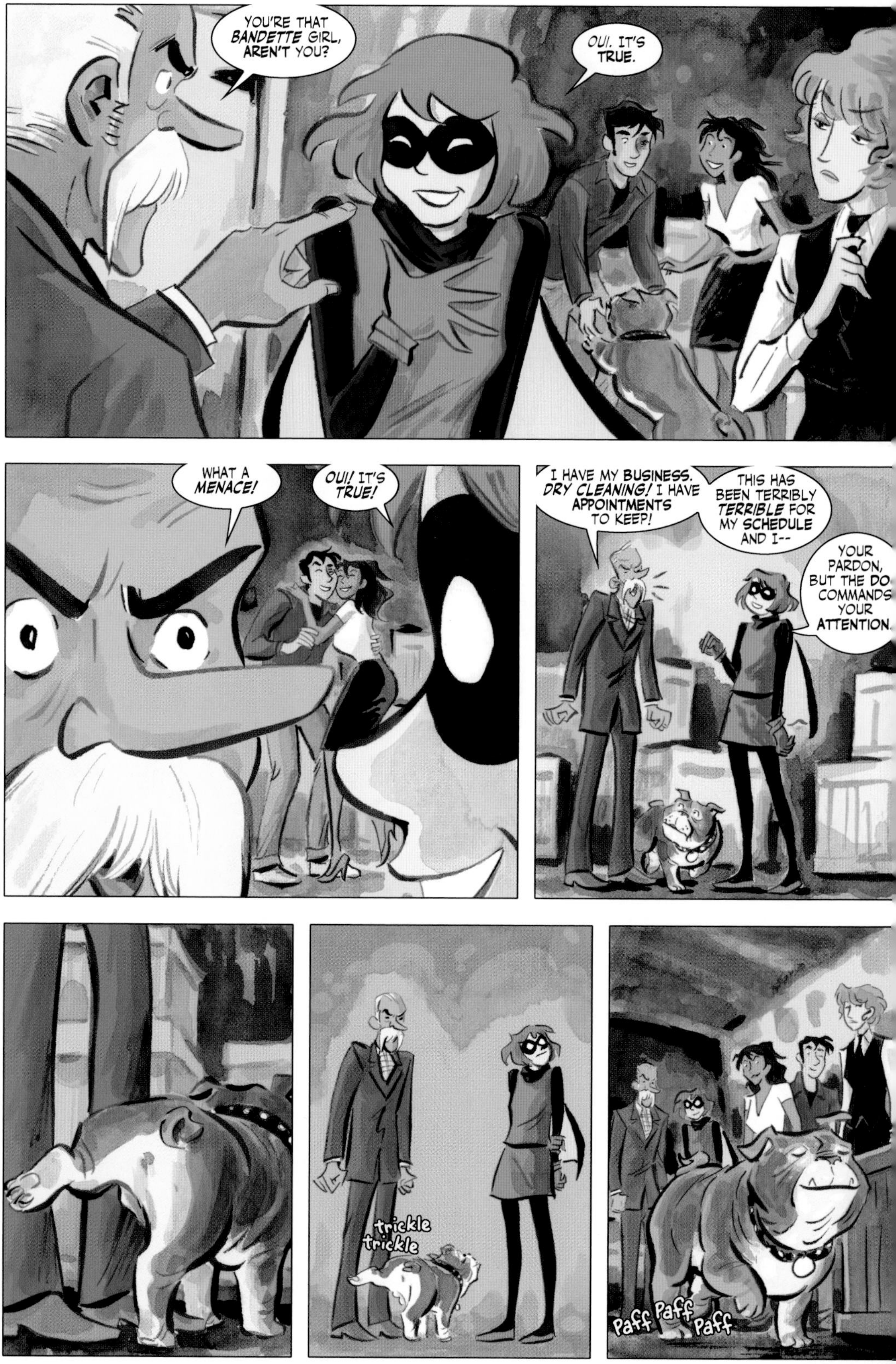
YOU'RE THAT BANDETTE GIRL, AREN'T YOU?
OUI. IT'S TRUE.
WHAT A MENACE!
OUI! IT'S TRUE!
I HAVE MY BUSINESS. DRY CLEANING! I HAVE APPOINTMENTS TO KEEP!
THIS HAS BEEN TERRIBLY TERRIBLE FOR MY SCHEDULE AND I--
YOUR PARDON, BUT THE DO COMMANDS YOUR ATTENTION.
trickle trickle
Paff Paff Paff

IT IS GOOD YOU HAVE DRY CLEANING, NO?

BANDETTE! I'M ABAGAIL SOVE!

THANKS *SO MUCH* TO YOU AND DANIEL FOR SAVING US!

BANDETTE.

hug hug HUG

I AM CASSANDRA. THIRD DAUGHTER OF THE MOON'S FULL EYE.

A PROTECTOR OF THE JADE MASK.

FOR THIS RESCUE, YOU HAVE MY GRATITUDE.

BUT I MUST WARN YOU...IF THIS IS SOME RUSE TO--

ONE MOMENT, IF YOU PLEASE.

OH...I... I NEVER KNEW.

THIS...

ALL THIS BUSINESS...

IT'S BEEN WORTH IT JUST TO SEE...

!

?

MEANWHILE...

GRRR.

BARK BARK!

RUFF! BARK!

RUFF! RUFF! BARK! RUFF!

dash dash scurry

BARK BARK BARK BARK!!

??

RUMBLE RUMBLE RUMBLE

87

RRRRROOAAAARR!!!

!

YIPE!

YIPP!

YIPE!

YIPE!

SWOOP!

PRESTO!

?

NOW WE ARE AIRBORNE.

I HAVE ATTACHED THIS ROPE TO A GIANT WOMAN. YOU HAVE HER TO THANK FOR YOUR RESCUE.

AND NOW, THE CHASE!

EXCUSE US, CHARMING MADEMOISELLES!

PIMENTO AND I ARE IN A CHASE!

EEE!

WHAT AN ADORABLE DOG!

OOO!

I LIKE HER MASK!

DO I SMELL CHOCOLATE?

OH?

YOUR PARDON, VARIOUS TALL MEN!

WE ARE CHASING A NEFARIOUS SCOUNDREL!

EEE!

WHERE IS THIS SCOUNDREL?

SHOULD WE HELP?

AHEAD, PIMENTO! WE MUST HURRY!

I MUST SINCERELY APOLOGIZE FOR MY HASTE!

YOU MUST TRUST THAT MY REASONS ARE VALID!

GOSCINNY'S PAPER BANNERS
Red for Love! · Blue for Friendship!
Green for Mystery! · Yellow if you love a parade!

THAP THAP THAP

EERRRTT!!

VVRRRNN!

BANDETTE! ONE MOMENT!

WE HAVE NEW CANDIES! JUST NOW IN STOCK!

SOME OTHER TIME, NOBLE CONFECTIONER!

BANDETTE IS IN A DRAMA!

UDERZO'S CANDIES

VVROOMM

BANDETTE! THE VOICE!

HE'S JUST TURNED THE CORNER! GETTING AWAY!

OH?

YIP!

VOILÀ!

THE SHORTCUT!

WE HAVE CORNERED HIM!

BRACE YOURSELF, MY PIMENTO. THE BATTLE IS ABOUT TO--

OH?

TOSS!

WOOOOSSHH!!

SSSSSSSSSS

!

SSSSSSSSSS

YIP! YIP! GRRRR!

CLANK!

HMMM.

THE DRAMA HAS ESCALATED.

SSSSSSSSSSSS

YIP! GRRR!

TAP TAP TAP

SIT!

SSSSSSSSSSSS

SSSSSSSSSSSS

GRAB!

SSSSSSSSSSSS

STAY!

OH?

EEE!

YOUR PARDON ONCE MORE, VARIOUS TALL MEN!

DID YOU FIND YOUR SCOUNDREL?

IS THAT...A BOMB?

SSSSSSSSSSSSS

AHHH, CHARMING MADEMOISELLES, A THIEF MUST PASS!

OOO!

SSSSSSSSSS

EEE!

I WANT A CAPE, TOO!

I DO SMELL CHOCOLATE! I AM SURE OF IT!

90

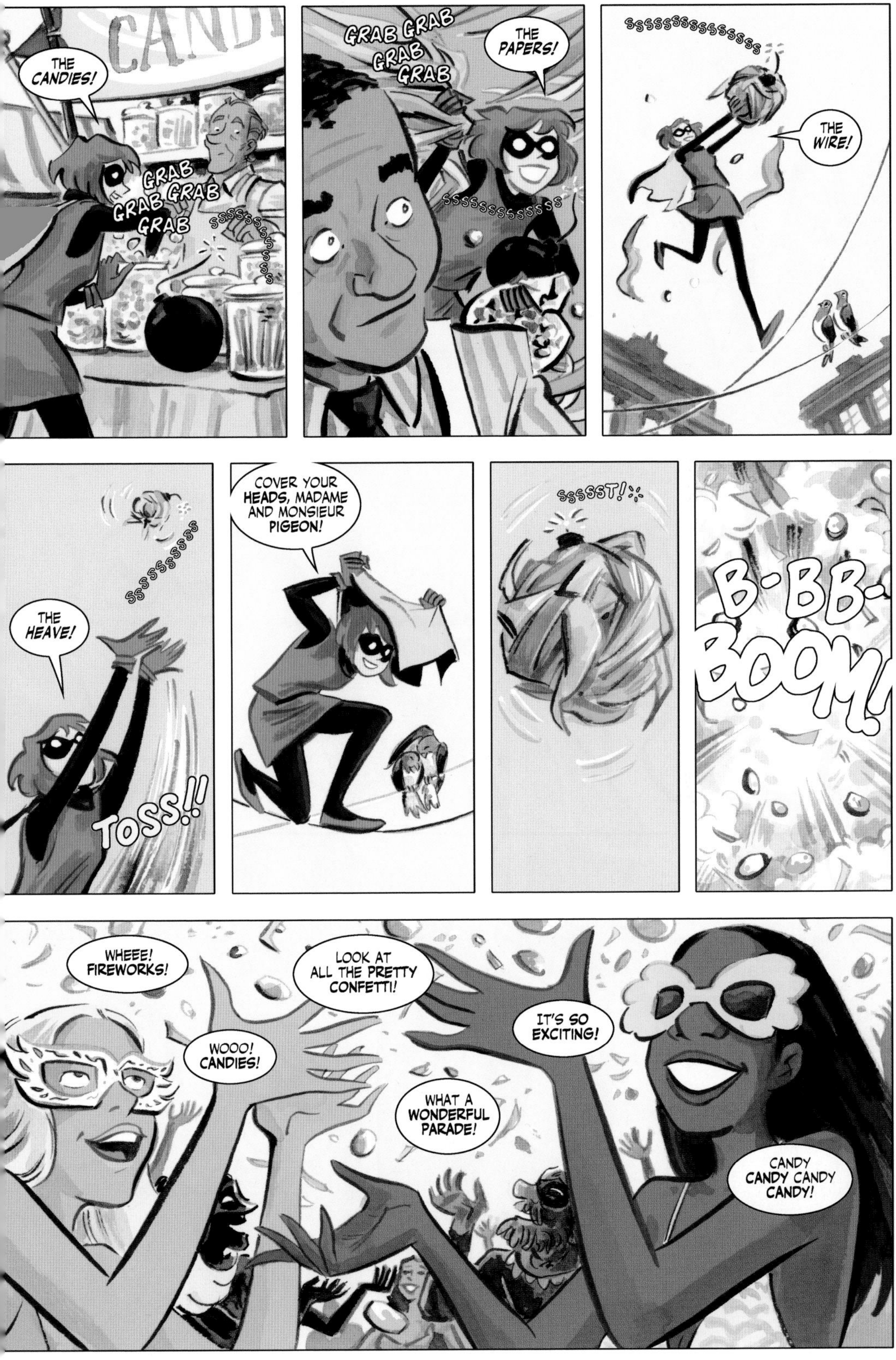

CANDI
THE CANDIES!
GRAB GRAB GRAB GRAB
SSSSSSSSS
GRAB GRAB GRAB GRAB
THE PAPERS!
SSSSSSSSSSSSSS
SSSSSSSSSSSSSSS
THE WIRE!
SSSSSSSSSS
THE HEAVE!
TOSS!!
COVER YOUR HEADS, MADAME AND MONSIEUR PIGEON!
SSSSST!
B-BB-BOOM!
WHEEE! FIREWORKS!
LOOK AT ALL THE PRETTY CONFETTI!
IT'S SO EXCITING!
WOOO! CANDIES!
WHAT A WONDERFUL PARADE!
CANDY CANDY CANDY CANDY!

pfff

ringg
ringg
ringg

BELGIQUE HERE.

IT IS *I*, BANDETTE! THE WORLD'S GREATEST THIEF!

ONCE **MORE** I STAND BEHIND YOU.

AT THE TIME OF OUR **EARLIER** DISCUSSION, I NEGLECTED TO MENTION THAT THIS BUILDING IS *STUFFED* WITH BOTHERSOME CRIMINALS AND THEIR WEAPONS.

PLEASE MAKE MANY ARRESTS.

SWIFF
SWIFF
SWIFF

ELSEWHERE...

THIS IS IT. I'VE FOUND IT!

THE HOUSE OF THE GREEN MASK.

LOOK! ABOVE THE DOOR.

IT SEEMS IN GOOD REPAIR FOR A TREASURE HOUSE THAT HAS BEEN UNDISTURBED FOR MORE THAN A HUNDRED YEARS.

YES. ODD, THAT. AND I THINK I HEAR...

...MUSIC?

WELCOME! WELCOME!

MADEMOISELLE MARGOT AND MONSIEUR MONSIEUR, YOUR TABLE IS WAITING!

AHH, BUT OF COURSE.

I WAS TOLD YOU MIGHT BE RATHER MYSTIFIED. THERE ARE UNDOUBTEDLY QUESTIONS TO BE ANSWERED.

MY NAME IS SHROPSHIRE WARRINGTON-YORK. I'LL BE YOUR ATTENDANT FOR THE EVENING.

THE MUSIC IS MOZART'S DIVERTIMENTO IN D MAJOR, K. 136, FROM THE SALZBURG SYMPHONIES

YOUR ENTRÉE IS FETTUCCINE CON OVOLI, PARMIGIANO, E TARTUFO BIANCO.

IT IS SERVED WITH A FINE WINE-- DOMAINE RAMONET MONTRACHET GRAND CRU--A SELECTION OF PETITS PAINS À L'AIL, AND FINALLY...

...THIS BASKET OF CHOCOBOLIK CANDY BARS.

I HAVE BEEN INSTRUCTED TO NOW PLACE THIS PHONE ON THE TABLE, AND THEN TO WITHDRAW FOR A MOMENT.

BONSOIR AND GOOD EVENING!

IT IS I, BANDETTE, THE WORLD'S MOST TALENTED THIEF!

OUI. I SUSPECTED AS MUCH.

94

I HOPE YOU'VE HAD A PLEASANT TIME SEARCHING FOR THE HOUSE OF THE GREEN MASK.

ALAS, MY DEAR *MONSIEUR,* AS YOU HAVE NOW SURMISED, THE TASK IS FUTILE.

THE IDENTITY OF THE GREAT LOVER, THE *MUSE* OF SO MANY ARTISTS, THE *INSPIRATION* FOR SO MANY RICHES... SHE MUST REMAIN SECRET.

IT IS MORE ROMANTIC THAT WAY, *NO?*

IT IS PERHAPS AT THIS MOMENT THAT YOUR STOMACH *ROILS,* YOUR FISTS CLENCH AT THE THOUGHT OF HAVING SO GREAT A TREASURE SLIP THROUGH YOUR *FINGERS,* BUT...

...BANDETTE HAS NOT *ONLY* PROVIDED YOU WITH AN EVENING FILLED WITH *CANDY BARS.* SHE IS ABOUT TO GIVE YOU THE *GREATEST* OF WISDOMS.

MONSIEUR, I TELL YOU *THIS...*

...THE *GREATEST* OF *ALL* TREASURES SITS AT THE *TABLE* WITH YOU.

SHROPSHIRE, YOU MAY POUR THE WINE.

MEANWHILE...

INSPECTOR? BANDETTE HAS TOLD ME THAT *THE VOICE* HAS **ESCAPED.** HE'S GOTTEN CLEAN AWAY.

YOU DON'T... YOU DON'T SEEM TO BE AS...**ANGRY** AS I THOUGHT YOU WOULD.

NO. I SUPPOSE NOT.

IT'S **TRUE** THAT I'M **SEETHING** INSIDE...

...AND THAT I WANT TO KICK DOWN SOME $/&#÷ DOORS, AND THROTTLE SOME ¡Ω#ΣΣ NECKS, AND SLAP SOME π*β#@ FACES, BUT...

...NOT LONG AGO WE WEREN'T EVEN SURE THE VOICE **EXISTED.**

NOW, NOT ONLY CAN WE **PROVE** HE IS REAL, BUT WE ALMOST **CAUGHT** HIM.

OF COURSE, IT'S *LIKEWISE* TRUE THAT THE VOICE IS NOW AWARE THAT WE'RE **ON** TO HIM.

SO WE HOLD A TIGER BY THE TAIL.

NOT AN **ENVIABLE** POSITION, I ADMIT.

BUT AT LEAST WE KNOW THE TIGER EXISTS, AND PERHAPS CAN BE DEFEATED, SO LONG AS WE NEVER LET GO OF THAT TAIL.

"SO LONG AS WE HOLD ON **TIGHT** TO WHAT WE DESIRE, AND **NEVER** LET IT GO."

BANDETTE WILL CONTINUE!

Urchin Stories

Written by Paul Tobin

B.D. Belgique in The Dogs

BY PAUL TOBIN
& STEVE LIEBER

JABBER JABBER EVIDENCE.

JABBER JABBER FINIS.

JABBER JABBER MURDER.

JABBER JABBER DRUGS.

JABBER JABBER CASE FILES.

JABBER JABBER PROSTITUTION.

JABBER JABBER ROBBERY.

BARK BARK BARK BARK

BARK BARK BARK

BARK BARK BARK BARK

BARK BARK BARK BARK BARK

BARK BARK BARK BARK

BARK BARK BARK BARK

BARK BARK BARK

ENOUGH! I CAN'T TAKE THIS!

THEY'RE LIKE *DOGS!* CONSTANTLY YAPPING! PEEING!

BELGIQUE! YOU NEED A *DAY OFF!*

AT THE BEACH!

OH, YOU BIG, STRONG MAN! WILL YOU DO POOR MIMI A FAVOR, YES?

HUH? BUT WHAT...?

I WISH TO SWIM, BUT I HAVE THE DOGS, NO?

THEN YOU...

WATCH THEM FOR ME, YES?

MERCI BEAUCOUP, MONSIEUR BIG NOSE!

I CANNOT POSSIBLY...

BUT... MADAM, I...YOU SEE, I...

BARK BARK BARK BARK

YAP YAP YAP YAP YAP YAP YPE YAP YI YAP YAP YAP YAP YA YAP

BARK BARK BARK BARK BARK BARK BARK

AHHH. C'EST LA VIE.

THE END

100

A Bandette "Urchin Story" featuring Heloise in...

"To Hire a Thief"

STORY
Paul Tobin

ART
Cat Farris

THIEF WANTED
Discretion a **MUST!**
Contact **Heloise**

I'M HERE.

OH!

UMMM, BANDETTE... I NEED YOU TO...STEAL SOMETHING.

BUT OF COURSE, HELOISE.

BUT, AS YOU KNOW, THERE IS A PRICE FOR COMMITTING A CRIME.

ARE YOU WILLING TO PAY?

THE NEXT DAY. SPECIAL POLICE HEADQUARTERS. 12:34 P.M.

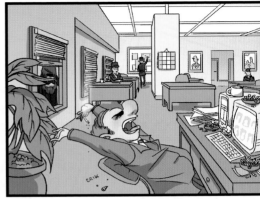

OUT OF COFFEE? #&@&!

NINE HOURS LATER.

SUCCESS! I HAVE DONE AS YOU ASKED.

IT'S JUST... THEY'RE NO GOOD FOR HIM.

OUI OUI! I AGREE. I AGREE. I WOULD HAVE DONE THIS FOR FREE.

NO, I'M HAPPY TO PAY YOUR USUAL PRICE.

HERE. A BOX OF CHOCOBOLIK CANDY BARS.

C'EST EXCELLENT! THIS WILL GO IN MY SAFE.

AND BY "MY SAFE" I MEAN "MY STOMACH."

FAREWELL, HELOISE. YOU ARE A GOOD WOMAN.

SIGH

IF ONLY, THIS TIME, THIS WOULD WORK.

103

CRIMINAL INTENT; OR, THE TERROR OF BAIT'S HOLLOW

This story of a village in the grips of a very peculiar crime spree is not a Bandette story, but it explores many of the same themes: mischief, mystery, and the stealing of hearts. It was one of Paul's first explorations of a whimsical thief and served as one of his many inspirations for the presto-wielding thief Bandette!

"Criminal Intent; or, The Terror of Bait's Hollow" first appeared in 2006 in the anthology *Papercutter* #2, edited by Greg Means and published by Tugboat Press.

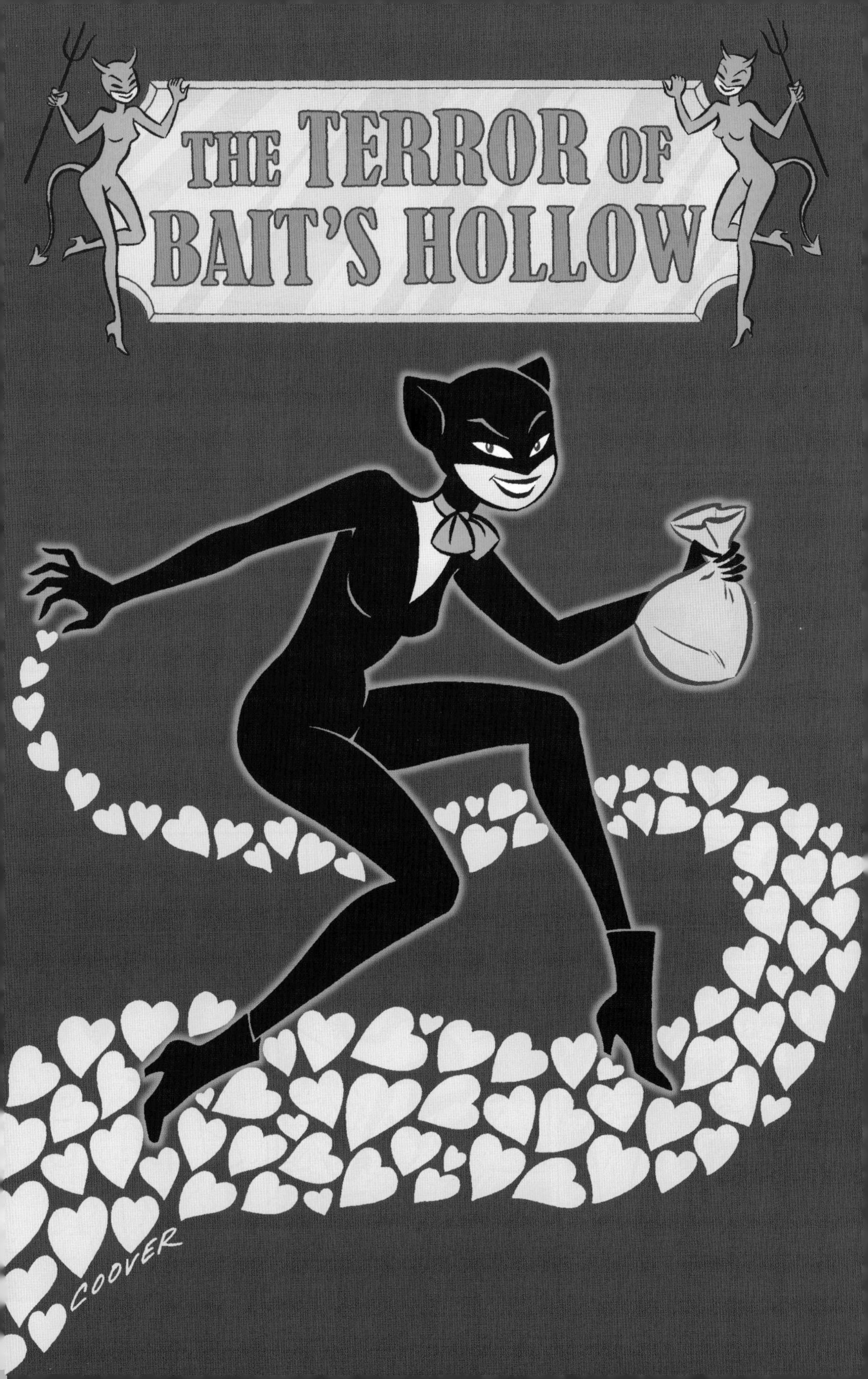
THE TERROR OF
BAIT'S HOLLOW
COOVER

CRIMINAL INTENT

A SLINKING MYSTERY

STORY: Paul Tobin
ART: Colleen Coover

Beginning in the sweltering summer of 1937, an audacious crime wave plagued the village of Bait's Hollow.

A slinking villainess reportedly struck a large number of households, betraying no preference for wealth or social standing.

Several pub attendees were waylaid and fleeced.

The local constabulary were severely taxed...not least because members of the force had fallen victim as well.

Jewels and other fine goods were often freely offered to the brazen thief, and so were not numbered among the purloined possessions.

The real losses were the many stolen hearts. Some victims reported that the thief had been so cruel as to whisk away their very souls.

The thief was relentless. Unstoppable.

The poor unfortunates who had fallen prey often differed in their accounts. Some told tales of heated feelings, others of a chilling cold.

What remains certain: these crimes could not have been purely human in origin.

The supernatural was at play.

Witness the curious story of Neville Collinsdown. For several weeks the poor soul envisioned his tormentor at every turn.

She took the guise of every man, woman, and child. Poor Neville could not banish the thief from his sight.

Nor could he reconcile the loss of his heart.

He was driven mad.

And the crime wave continued... Not even shamed into temporary abeyance by this tragedy.

The thief, unchecked as she was by walls or strong hearts, was clearly a demon in disguise. Suspicion therefore naturally fell upon outsiders.

Speculation fell chiefly on the *Manoir des Triplés*, the abode of three sisters who had recently relocated from France to Bait's Hollow. Were they conjurers, or perhaps fabulists?

Several intrepid citizens risked all while gathering information on these lovely enchantresses.

Most returned changed men, and took heavily to drink.

Illegible

This turn to spirits was a dangerous proposition...

The crimes continued. The thief soon held sway over the entire valley.

Men woke shuddering in their beds, certain the villainess had marked them.

They staggered along midnight walkways, fearing for their safety.

Eventually, even women and schoolchildren succumbed to the unrelenting felonious assault.

Bait's Hollow, sad town, was utterly plundered.

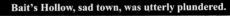

Were the French sisters truly to blame? Who can say?

It is folly, of course, to ascribe human explanations to supernatural manifestations.

Despite the many intervening years, the police of Bait's Hollow still receive fresh reports of absconded hearts.

The preternatural thief, against whom no locked door or proud chest could prove a sufficient obstacle, has now skipped daintily past the curtain of time.

No treasured heart remains safe. No soul can be counted as beyond her reach.

AND PERHAPS YOURS WILL BE NEXT.

END

THE MUSIC

By Paul Tobin
Illustrations by Colleen Coover

Heloise stopped at the commissary for a slice of carrot cake.

It was indulgent, she knew, but the carrot cake in the lunchroom for the Special Police Forces was the best she'd ever encountered, better even than those slices served at the Salon Café on the rue de Grand Guignol, the ones lightly sprinkled with manchego cheese—so delicious when paired with a glass of white wine and the latest romance novel by Melisande Goncourt, who penned stories of police procedurals and hidden clues, starring gruff men who barreled their way through the roughest of criminals as if they were nothing more than tenpins, but who ultimately found themselves at the mercy of some woman's love.

There was the slightest clink of her fork when she speared it down through the cake with such vitality and vigor that it hit the plate beneath.

Heloise relished that sound. It had impact. It had meaning. It was not unlike that bell rung by Pavlov to signal his dogs, the mere ringing of the bell prompting the hounds to drool in anticipation of an expected treat. Whenever Heloise ate carrot cake she thought of that particular sound, that musical *tinggg* of her fork hitting her plate, and she wondered if that noise—properly recorded—could make her salivate.

Probably.

Most likely.

She was such a creature of habit.

Which was partially why she was so relishing this miniature act of rebellion. This stopover at the commissary. This carrot cake. When her boss, Inspector B. D. Belgique, had given her the sealed plastic bag containing the diary of the bank robber, telling her to take it straightaway to the evidence room and personally enter it into the proper file, he'd of course expected Heloise to rush rush rush—her heels clicking on the basement's concrete floors—in order to complete the task with all speed and efficiency.

But here, now, there was this silliness with the carrot cake. She was blushing. She'd needed a moment to herself. It was because in the midst of all the odious swearing with which Belgique peppered his everyday conversation, between her fascination for the way his bulbous nose squished and squinched with his every bellowed word, she'd been watching his lips when they blew clouds of cigarette smoke almost right into her face, which was rude, of course.

Of course it was rude.

But she found herself savoring the rich, earthy smell of the smoky scent that had seeped into her clothes. The scent reminded her of so many things. Raking her great-aunt's lawns during the fall. Playing in the haylofts of her grandfather's vineyards just outside Ille-sur-Tet, in the barn with the three brown-eyed cows he'd kept ever since the American western movies had convinced him that he needed to be a "proper" farmer.

Gruff men who barreled their way through the roughest of criminals as if they were nothing more than tenpins.

These were the memories that Belgique's cheap cigarettes brought back, and so Heloise had decided to spend a few moments publicly savoring the taste of the carrot cake while more privately savoring the aroma still trapped in the dark blue cloth of her uniform. It was strangely romantic, Heloise thought, to be surrounded by her fellow officers on their lunch breaks, sitting in this commissary in the middle of the city, and yet with a simple turn of her head and a slight sniff of her nose she could inhale the remnants of cigarette smoke and be transported to that autumn lawn strewn with leaves, the sound of the rake scraping across the grass, gathering the leaves, freshening their scent. The simplest whiff of Belgique's smoke, and Heloise was climbing up the ladder to her grandfather's haylofts, her skirts swishing around her young legs, the heady scent of the hay filling her lungs, the dance of the particles caught in the beams of sunlight coming through the window, motes of dust disturbed by the barking breath of her laughter as she used a pitchfork to fling bundles of hay down to the pen below, to where the cows accepted this gift with the dull notice of their kind, barely glancing up to the teenaged girl with hay in her hair. One simple sniff of the cigarette smoke still caught in the fabric of her uniform, and Heloise could recall the sound of Belgique's voice, that underlying power that made her shiver, the smoke a seeming manifestation of his breath, the strength of his presence and the command of his voice, the one that always sent her heart barreling along with an exquisite thrill of—

"Hello, Heloise!" came a voice.

"No!" she grunted, a bit loud, or . . . in fact . . . a bit more than a bit loud.

"No . . . what?" Heloise heard, looking up to find Sylvia, the chef, standing next to her table. Sylvia's face held an expression of confusion, and Heloise felt herself coloring, an unfortunately commonplace occurrence of late.

Playing in the haylofts of her grandfather's vineyards just outside Ille-sur-Tet, in the barn with the three brown cows.

"Sorry," Heloise said. "My thoughts were drifting. Hello, Sylvia. This cake is marvelous today." She slid her fork through the carrot cake, clinking it into the plate and then holding up a bit of the cake as if to show Sylvia, who most likely had already seen it . . . Heloise realized . . . as the chef had baked it, after all.

"I'll consider your current lack of mental abilities as sufficient praise for my culinary skills," Sylvia said. She then nudged the diary in the sealed plastic bag where it lay beside Heloise's plate and asked, "What's this?"

"Evidence. A bank robber's diary. A detailed plan. It needs to be filed. I was just on my way."

"Oh. Belgique's having you file? That explains things. You smell like his cigarettes, you know."

"Good," Heloise said, all without thinking, and then she colored again.

"Good?" Sylvia asked, looking closer at Heloise, leaning in to stare deep into her eyes. There was a heartbeat of time and then Sylvia smiled, emphatically nodded, and said, "Ahh, yes. There it is. That explains it. Belgique. That man. That commanding voice. No wonder you're always so breathless of late."

"I have no idea what you're talking about," Heloise said, gathering up her dishes and hurriedly putting them into the tub for the dishwashers, clutching the criminal's diary to her chest and scampering away, her heels clicking on the floor, cursing herself for once more blushing.

．．．．．．．．．．．．．．．．．．．

There were three doors to pass through before entering the evidence room. Well, two doors and one gate. The first door required a keycard and a nine-digit code. The second needed the keycard again, plus a quick word with the attendant, who scrutinized every face and every ID card, no matter how many times he'd seen them before. Passage though that second door led Heloise to a room with the third barrier: the barred gates to the evidence room. Two guards sat at desks to either side of the gate, which would open only when the guard on the left used her key in the mechanism set into the wall behind her chair, while the guard to the right simultaneously held down a combination of keystrokes on his computer. Above their desks

Heloise felt herself coloring, an unfortunately commonplace occurrence of late.

and scattered through the small room were seven security cameras running through three different systems in case of any computer failure. Altogether, the evidence lockup was the most secure room Heloise had ever seen, owing to the vast collection of material contained in what amounted to an entire warehouse beyond the gates: a treasure trove of evidence that reached back, in some cases, well over a century in the past. Heloise, clutching the diary to her chest, was about to add to that vast storehouse.

Altogether, the evidence lockup was the most secure room Heloise had ever seen.

"Row M," she said to herself after she signed in and the gate was buzzed open. She walked through the aisles, glancing at the numbers and the letters at the ends of each row, the sturdy metal shelves with their boxes and their crates, their folders and their peculiar and sometimes frightening objects: murder weapons of an amazing variety, photographs of crime scenes,

boxes of victims' clothing, taped recordings of confessions, plaster casts of tire tracks. The only noises in the room were the echoing click of Heloise's heels and the steady hum of the air conditioner. The latter kept the room at a fixed temperature several degrees too cold for Heloise, so that she was forever shivering while in the small warehouse, but she enjoyed the machine's hum because it reminded her of the ocean and its subtle roar. She also enjoyed the scent inside the evidence room, because there was no scent at all. The air filters stole everything away, leaving the air crisp and cold, like a winter's morning, with the aroma of falling snow, which Heloise believed had no smell at all, but somehow . . . at the same time . . . she could still recognize it at the merest whiff. It was a clean scent. An aroma of purity, of open spaces, of . . . of . . .

Strawberries.

Heloise smelled strawberries.

Rounding the corner of an aisle, curiously following the scent of strawberries, Heloise nearly tripped over the girl on the floor.

It was a girl who was both friend and nemesis to the Special Police Forces.

It was a girl who was spreading a picnic blanket over the concrete floor, with a wicker basket set to one side, partially open to reveal cakes and candies and a carton of plump ripe strawberries.

It was a girl munching on a candy bar.

It was a thief.

It was Bandette.

• •

Altogether, the evidence lockup was the most secure room Heloise had ever seen.

"Ahh, you have arrived," Bandette said. "We can get down to business, then, no?"

Heloise smelled strawberries.

"W-what?" Heloise stuttered. "Business? What business? And . . . you can't be here."

"I must be here," Bandette said, looking around as if to make sure. "For I am currently in no other places, so by simple means of elimination, this is where I must be, yes? Do you like strawberries, Heloise?"

"No."

"This cannot be true!" Bandette said, springing to her feet. "Strawberries are delicious, and they go quite well with candy bars. Though, to be sure, all things go well with candy bars, even . . . and perhaps especially . . . more candy bars."

"I do like strawberries," Heloise said. "But I meant that, no, you can't be here. How did you get in here?" Heloise was looking quickly around, trying to spot some doorway she'd missed, some new entrance that her superiors had forgotten to mention.

"But I came through the door," Bandette said, as if the several layers of security were not even worthy of mention. Heloise was restraining herself from grabbing up the checkered picnic cloth and tossing it over the thief's head in hopes of hiding her, in hopes of somehow keeping the secret, in hopes of never hearing why Bandette had been so foolish as to come into the evidence storeroom with the picnic basket full of pastries and strawberries and candy bars, which Bandette was now spreading out on the floor as

if arranging for a feast, pouring glasses of water and setting them next to . . . to . . .

. . . an evidence folder.

"What are you doing with *that*?" Heloise said, pointing to the folder, which looked old. It had several stains. Yellowing papers. It was a file that was inches thick, and it had no business being in the hands of Bandette. For while Heloise considered the thief to be her friend, and while Bandette had been instrumental in so many cases of art recovery, and of course she'd helped to topple FINIS and Absinthe, it was beyond the realm of propriety for anyone . . . let alone a thief . . . to be carelessly rifling through the files and folders in the evidence room. Heloise knew, in that moment, that the thief had gone too far. And so it was with great sorrow . . . but with a greater sense of purpose and loyalty to the code of honor to which she'd sworn while accepting the uniform . . . that Heloise decided she would have to arrest Bandette.

"This?" Bandette said, flopping in almost bone-less fashion down to the floor, tapping on the file with the end of an unwrapped candy bar, leaving the slightest smear of chocolate. "This is the file from the very first case of a then-young B. D. Belgique. This is a case that was never solved." Another tap with the candy bar, which was now shorter, as Bandette had chomped off an impressive amount in one bite. "This is a file regarding a missing sword, stolen from the mansion of a film producer and never recovered, so that our Monsieur Belgique began his career with a stumble, a trip, a stagger, and a slip."

Heloise could think of nothing to say. She only watched as the thief finished her candy bar and then plucked the stems from three strawberries before tossing the juicy red fruits into her mouth as though they were popcorn, one after the other, chomping with great relish while opening the wrapper for a second candy bar, or perhaps a third or fourth. Heloise had lost count, so

It was a girl who was spreading a picnic blanket over the concrete floor. It was a thief. It was Bandette.

astonished was she at finding Bandette in the evidence room and so occupied with worry over how much commotion would be caused when she, Heloise, escorted the teenage thief down to the holding cells in handcuffs.

"This sword," Bandette said, opening the file and pointing to a photo of a Chinese sword. It was beautiful and ancient, with pierced brass fittings along its pommel and cross guard, delicate images of tiny rearing horses sculpted in the metal. The grip was wrapped in rich urple cloth, and the blade was dark, shining steel. The scabbard was even more elegantly crafted, with a continuation of the pierced brass and horse motif, plus finely fitted jade plaques that seemed almost to glow, even in the photo. Next to this photo was an image of a youthful B. D. Belgique inspecting the scene of a crime, pointing to some clue on the floor. His face was years younger, leaner, freshly shaven, and slightly pink, filled with the energy of youth but

also—Heloise thought—somewhat less of the confidence he now had. The assurance was still there in his eyes, but the arrogance was not. Arrogance was not something to be countenanced in a man, of course, but Heloise felt that B. D. had earned a right to his arrogance and often found herself not quite thrilled, but at least excited, to be in its path.

"It is this very sword," Bandette said, nimbly tapping on the photo with her toe while putting a custard tart on a plate, "that I have recently seen while having an innocent midnight stroll through a certain mansion—a mansion to which I quite doubt the police could ever possibly obtain a search warrant. Would it not be amusing if two women were to some-how, by some means, gain entry into this house? Recover the sword? To solve this lingering mystery of Belgique's first case and see if there might not be, hidden somewhere in his gruff voice, a word of gratitude? This would be amusing, no?"

Heloise had nothing to say.

Nothing.

She found herself with her lips tightly closed. She found herself heaving her breaths at an uncertain pace. She found herself sitting down on the checkered cloth and accepting a plate holding a custard tart, with a fork and straw-berries and a candy bar to one side.

• • • • • • • • • • • • • • • • • • • •

Heloise stared at herself in the mirror, or at least stared at the person who was being reflected in the mirror, because it hardly seemed possible that she was looking at herself. The person in the mirror was wearing a black bodysuit, a

"This is a case that was never solved."

short red cape with matching red slippers, and a red mask that made her appear to be some kind of criminal.

"I can't do this," she whispered, but Bandette merely tapped her finger on the photo of the Chinese sword she'd stuck to the mirror in the upper left, and then she tapped a finger on the photo of the young B. D. Belgique in the other corner.

"Do not disappoint this man," Bandette said. "His heart will be broken. It would snap like a twig when a hippopotamus leaps upon it, like so!" The nimble thief began, apparently, to mimic the actions of a leaping hippopotamus, jumping about the room.

The room was in the clock tower that loomed over the markets in Pompadour Square, a clock tower that Heloise had believed abandoned for years before she and Bandette climbed a ladder, opened a window, and snuck inside. There, the thief had switched a lever hidden beneath the chin of a marble bust of Oscar Wilde, and a section of the dusty wall had . . . to Heloise's great surprise . . . opened to reveal an antique elevator. Together, they had ascended into the clock tower, to an open room with an amazing

collection of art that the policewoman had immediately decided against scrutinizing, because the paintings and statues were undoubtedly stolen from an assortment of mansions and museums. The thief had led Heloise deeper into the clock tower, stepping over a restoration project for the clock itself, then past a row of Japanese screens to a fitting room of sorts. The space was filled with costumes of all types, the walls lined with standing mirrors in carved wooden frames. Heloise felt a fool trying on one outfit after another, as Bandette seemed to believe that the adventure at hand (and there was a looming adventure, a theft in the making) would be best served by a policewoman dressed as a seventeenth-century carriage driver, or perhaps an American astronaut.

Finally, the black bodysuit. It was not, Heloise felt, an outfit designed for a woman of her figure.

"And now," Bandette said. "The important lessons of thieving. First, confidence above all else. We begin by stealing from Pimento." The thief pointed to her Chihuahua, who was gnawing a bone on a rug in the middle of the floor. The dog looked up when he heard his name.

Bandette said, "I will give Pimento this original Picasso drawing of a dog gnawing on a bone. We have a theme, no? You will please steal it from him." Bandette, true to her word, leaned a framed drawing up against Pimento: a small drawing executed in bold strokes of ink, depicting some drool-jawed mastiff working on a bone. Pimento took no notice and simply kept working on his own bone, oblivious to the world's most talented thief teaching her art to . . . in Heloise's mind . . . the world's most ridiculous policewoman.

She took a step forward.

Pimento looked up, quizzical.

Heloise took another step.

Together, they had ascended into the clock tower.

The dog growled.

Heloise stopped.

"I can't do this," she found herself whispering. She turned to Bandette but found that the thief was ignoring her, putting a cylinder recording on an ancient Victrola record player. Soon the swinging sounds of heady jazz music were filling the clock tower, and Bandette was cartwheeling to her feet, bounding across the floor, somersaulting over disassembled clock parts, leaping off the back of a couch to grab a ceiling beam, flipping over to another beam, and running along in the dark recesses of the ceiling above before jumping down only inches away from Heloise, making the policewoman gasp in surprise. Then, before Heloise could react, the young girl was taking her by her hands, moving her to the center of the room, guiding her in a dance, swinging and swaying, always in motion, with Heloise stumbling after.

"The music," Bandette said. "Heloise, you must listen to the music."

"I can't possibly—" Heloise began, but Bandette's hand swooped up to cover Heloise's mouth before she could continue.

"We are not listening to you," Bandette said. "And we are not even listening to me. That would be silly, no? We will only listen to the music. We will not hear the sound of our voices, the seeds of any doubts, the sounds of our footsteps, or anything but the music inside this room, the music we all hold in our hearts. We will think of candy bars and the laughter of our friends. We will match our heartbeats to whatever music we choose, whatever dreams our fingers can touch. We will be silent, so that we can hear everything."

And all along, as Bandette spoke, she was leading Heloise in a dance, sweeping her over and around the room, past the paintings on the walls, past the statues on the floor, past the mirrors where Heloise could catch quick flashes of her reflection, the way she was moving, sped along

The person in the mirror was wearing a black bodysuit, a short red cape with matching red slippers, and a red mask that made her appear to be some kind of criminal.

so quickly, her breath so rapid, the brightness of Bandette's costume seeming almost to merge with the darkness of her own, the thief's balance always so precise, so graceful, that Heloise felt almost plodding, but she was nevertheless carried along, guided by a master until their movements began to mesh, to coincide, the music charging through Heloise's veins and into her heart, opening her memories of those days in Ille-sur-Tet, her grandfather's vineyards, the times they'd harvested together, the radio he'd always carried as they'd picked the grapes, with him singing along, his voice an atrocity that was simply wonderful, because there was so much joy inside, and Heloise could remember the times she'd sung along with his words, matching her voice to his own, the two of them stepping through the fields, carrying their baskets of grapes, dancing from one vine to another, her grandmother clapping in time, the grapes seeming to leap from the vines to her fingers, into her basket, Edith Piaf's voice on the radio singing of lost loves, discovered lovers, with Heloise not understanding the meaning but understanding the mood and of course how her grandfather had laughed and how the winds would sweep over the hills and rush down to see them. And all through these memories the thief Bandette was taking Heloise along with her over and around the clock tower room, as insistent and as capricious as the winds that blew through those vineyards, and Heloise found that she was laughing as Bandette made them dance on a couch, made them leap over the monstrous clock parts that were strewn about the room, no more stumbles, no more trips, no more hesitation, and it was all over too soon, far too soon, because Heloise could have danced forever, at least, or more.

But Bandette stopped her.

Guided her to a stop.

Heloise's breath caught up to her and she found that she was panting, heaving through a broad grin.

"Why have we stopped?" she asked.

In reply, Bandette only nodded to their clasped hands. Heloise looked and was surprised to discover she was holding a fine Picasso drawing of a large dog gnawing on a bone.

"I've stolen it?" Heloise gasped. "When did that happen?"

"What does that matter?" answered the thief.

. . . .

When Bandette and Heloise were going over the wall together, Heloise was thinking of the first and only time she'd ever tried smoking cigarettes.

"We will match our heartbeats to whatever music we choose, whatever dreams our fingers can touch."

It was in her second year of working for the Special Police Forces, and she'd been walking past a kiosk that sold water, magazines, newspapers, candies, postcards, and . . . cigarettes. There were, in fact, packs of Craymore cigarettes. Belgique's favored brand. Horrible things, in Heloise's mind. What could be the draw? She had to know. She'd found herself purchasing the cigarettes and then sitting next to the lake, watching lovers paddling about in the funny little boats shaped like ducks and swans and even a tiger. It had taken Heloise almost thirty minutes of mental preparation in order to take the first cigarette out from the pack, and then she'd sat for a further five minutes before she'd had the nerve to ask a passerby for a light, since she'd forgotten that she would also need matches.

The first inhalation had been abysmal. The smoke had slid down her throat like a snake wearing a sandpaper coat. She'd coughed for nearly a minute, hacking so vigorously that the couples in their boats had paddled away to the deeper recesses of the lake. The second inhalation was similar to the first, and the third was worse than the others, and she'd tossed the cigarette to the ground and stomped it flat with her shoe, meanwhile keeping several pigeons at bay, because the birds were curious as to whether the Craymore cigarette might be an interesting

Belgique's favored brand.

snack. She'd thrown the rest of the cigarettes away in the garbage.

Heloise had been trying to get Belgique to quit the disgusting habit ever since, but he was too stubborn, too caught in his ways, even as she argued with him about the terrible health problems and the simple monetary cost of cigarettes. She had all sorts of fantasies of how she would forbid Belgique, absolutely forbid him, to smoke in her apartment. He had never been to her apartment, but she had her fantasies.

"Wait here," Bandette said after they'd dashed stealthily across the lawns of the mansion where, according to the thief, the stolen Chinese sword was waiting. The young girl began scaling up the vines on the side of the darkened mansion, illuminated by the light of the full moon high in the sky. There was no sound as Bandette found her grip, as she planted her feet, not even a shiver of the leaves of creeping ivy as she scurried up the side of the building. Soon, she was out of sight, crawling in through a window that had either been left unlocked or otherwise coaxed to open.

Left alone to peer curiously into the darkened panes of a glass door that had decidedly not been left unlocked, Heloise was returning to her fantasies of Belgique's stammering apologies at having ever smoked a single cigarette, when she heard a rustling noise behind her. At first she merely frowned, wondering at how quickly Bandette always moved, at how secretive and silent she could be, at how the teenager had climbed up a wall in front of her and then down to the lawns behind her, all as mysteriously as how the thief had somehow appeared in the evidence warehouse of the Special Police Forces.

And so . . . with her thoughts lost in this manner . . . Heloise was not in the slightest bit prepared when she turned to find not Bandette, but instead three German shepherd guard dogs, teeth bared, rushing forward.

"Oh no," she whispered.

· ·

"Presto," Bandette said, stepping out of the door behind Heloise, having unlocked it from within. Then, the thief frowned as she saw how the night had progressed in the short time she'd been absent, with the dogs racing toward the wide-eyed Heloise, the policewoman shivering, the dogs snarling. Heloise sought the safety of the open doorway, desperately running two steps toward the mansion before Bandette, to Heloise's unbelieving eyes, turned and shut the door.

"No and alas," the thief told the oncoming dogs. "You must not come into the house. You would leave many tracks, yes? This cannot be." She stepped around Heloise and sprayed a mist from a tiny can. The first dog flopped to the lawn, snoring even as he tumbled to a stop.

"Knockout gas," the thief explained, turning to Heloise and displaying the small spray can. "Quite useful against ill-mannered pests." The next dog leapt for the thief's throat. Bandette ducked, rolled, and then . . . with a quick movement . . . landed on the dog's back, like one of those curious American cowboys.

"This horse is too small," Bandette said, frowning. There was another spritz of the spray can, and the dog sprawled to the grass even as Bandette rolled gracefully free, though unfortunately into the path of the remaining dog.

"Grrr," the dog said.

"Eek," Heloise whispered.

"Sniff," Bandette commanded, holding out her arm to a dog that looked quite likely to chomp it off in one bite. Instead, it prowled back and forth in front of Bandette, alert, menacing. It reminded Heloise very much of the dog that lived at her neighbor's house, a frightening black Labrador that spent its time growling at Heloise whenever she left in the morning, straining at the chain that kept it in place next to the walkway, snapping at the air with teeth that Heloise felt were several times too large for the dog, as if it had borrowed a shark's teeth in order to further her fright.

"Be careful, Bandette," Heloise said. "The dog is savage."

"I suppose," the thief said, though she clearly did not. She turned back to the dog and, with her voice full of mirth, pointed once more to her arm.

"Sniff," she said again, and the dog did indeed slink forward, and it did indeed sniff Bandette's arm, though with bared teeth, ready to bite at a moment's notice.

Then, the dog underwent a change. It straightened. Its tail began to wag. Its tongue lolled out.

"It is pleasant perfume, no?" Bandette told the dog, kneeling to scratch beneath his chin. "A mixture sold only in certain stores. A blend of fresh lilies and charred steak. I could send some around, if you would like. It might impress the lady dogs. Do you have opportunities to date, or are you too busy guarding this house?"

"Whuff," the dog said.

"Oh-ho!" Bandette replied. "You are a scoundrel. Heloise and I will leave you to your games, then, you rogue of women's hearts."

The thief hugged the dog, flipped up onto her feet, and grabbed Heloise's hand, and together they were through the door in moments.

· ·

"I thought I would faint when you hugged that horrifying dog," Heloise told Bandette as they moved down a hallway lit only by moonlight.

"But why?" Bandette asked.

"He was mean!"

"This is not true. Some dogs bark only because they need to be hugged. A simple clasp and they are puppies again."

"Oh," Heloise said, thinking of what the thief was saying, which was much better than thinking of the voices of the men she could hear in the surrounding rooms: the guards who were prowling the mansion, the guards Bandette was helping her to avoid.

Hiding behind a large potted plant, Heloise asked in a whisper, "Did you . . . did you really understand what that dog said?"

"I did not. Such things are impossible, I believe. Yes, I'm sure they are. Quite impossible. Or at the least very unlikely."

"But . . . you answered him when he spoke. Or when he barked, I mean."

"Of course I answered. Communication with a dog is about confidence. As thieving is about confidence. And love as well, if such matters might ever cross your mind. But we must be quiet here in this house, or we will be discovered."

The thief hugged the dog.

With that said, the young thief began humming out loud, occasionally singing as she made her way down a hallway that was lined with curio cabinets displaying rare coins and fabulous jewels, artifacts that Bandette was occasionally inspecting and, only slightly less occasionally, tucking into the pockets of her cape.

"We shouldn't steal anything!" Heloise said, aghast.

"Of course we shouldn't!" Bandette replied, equally aghast. "No, it is only I who should be stealing things." She tucked a diamond necklace into her cape. "Come now," she urged, tugging Heloise into a room. "Here is the sword!"

And indeed, there was the sword. Heloise had studied the file that Bandette had showed her in the evidence room, and . . . yes, here it was . . . the sword. The finely worked metals with the rearing horses. The green jade of the scabbard. The black metal of the blade itself, which was made of Damascus steel, according to the case file that Heloise had read. She'd also learned of how the young B. D. Belgique had investigated the blade's theft from the palatial home of a Chinese filmmaker who produced not only historical epics filled with fantastical martial arts (movies to which Bandette had given glowing reviews) but also a series of well-received documentaries on the cabaret culture of wartime China. The sword's theft had gone unsolved, primarily due to the influence of the key suspects: gangsters who'd had their hands . . . it was sad to say . . . in the pockets of several corrupt high-ranking policemen of the time.

And so Belgique's quest to recover the sword had failed.

But now, here it was, in a darkened room, in a fine glass display case, in front of Heloise, who was starting to itch in her black bodysuit.

She reached for the sword.

"Ah, *non non non*," Bandette scolded. "*Ne touchez pas.* Do not touch." She reached out to stay Heloise's hand, and then, with a quick movement, the teen lifted a thin cylindrical canister and sprayed a blue mist that gathered in the air to reveal a series of lasers flitting above and about the glass case.

"The alarm would sound," Bandette said with a shrug. "So vexing, these lasers. And there are also pressure pads, and heat sensors, and other scurrilous perils."

"What can we do?" Heloise asked.

"We must learn the code to enter into that keypad," Bandette answered, gesturing to a number pad on an opposite wall. "And only then can we safely remove the sword, and then also celebrate with two or three candy bars, if we are in a hurry, or perhaps more at our leisure."

"But how can we learn the proper code?" Heloise asked, whispering and shivering in the darkened room.

"It is most simple!" Bandette said. "We steal it!" She turned and brightly marched out of the room, which had rows of other weapons mounted upon the walls, not only a wide array of daggers and spears and still more swords, but also guns and rifles. The room smelled of oil, metal, and danger, and Heloise was only too glad to leave, at least until Bandette guided her into a new room, a bedroom, a private room, where a man was sleeping.

"Oh no," Heloise whispered, her words audible only to herself but seemingly far too loud despite that. But Bandette was simply creeping past the bed, walking with exaggerated care as if she were a character in some farce, rather than a teenaged thief walking past a bed where Gilles Sauvage . . . the notorious local leader of the Milieu . . . the lord of organized crime known, rather obviously, as the Savage . . . was

sleeping. This was a man who was suspected of several murders, arsons, thefts, base crimes of all kinds. His photo had been included in the young B. D. Belgique's reports of the sword's theft, which was how Heloise was so easily able to identify the man even now, even in the dark, even as he was older, even as he was slumbering in his pajamas atop the bed, snoring with gusto, perhaps the most dangerous man in the city, with one gun on his nightstand and another peeking out from beneath his pillow.

"Oh no," Heloise whispered again, watching Bandette, the young thief, leaping up onto the bed.

Heloise could not take a step.

Bandette, on the bed, was stepping over the sleeping man.

Heloise could not take a breath.

Bandette was removing a painting from the wall above the crime lord, leaning it against the headboard only inches from the slumbering Savage.

"*Ne touchez pas.*"

123

Heloise could not so much as blink.

Bandette was working at the dial of a safe that had been revealed once the painting was removed. Her movements were quick, deft, and she seemed to be listening to some inner music, almost dancing on the bed, slightly shifting the mattress, whispering "Presto!" as the safe swung open.

Heloise could feel the sweat trickling down her back.

Bandette was helping herself to a selection of items from within the safe, munching on a candy bar while picking and choosing small items such as rare coins and fabulous jewels that all seemed to wink in the moonlight, at least until they were hidden inside the thief's cape. Then, Bandette reached into the safe and pulled out a small red book, waving it at Heloise, who stood at the foot of the bed as if she were an iron statue that had somehow . . . as if in some absurd fairy tale . . . gained the ability to sweat.

"I have found this!" Bandette said. "Certainly this is where the code will be written!" She was

Bandette was removing a painting from the wall above the crime lord, only inches from the slumbering Savage.

stepping over the sleeping man, who was stirring, shifting, so that Bandette was having to change her balance in order to avoid him.

"Like a cat, this man!" said the thief. "Always underfoot!" Heloise was still in shock over the first time Bandette had spoken, still urging her trembling muscles to bring her finger to her mouth to shush the young girl, but by the time Heloise could manage this Herculean feat, Bandette had moved to the edge of the bed and leapt into the air, flipping once before landing silently on her feet, taking Heloise by the arm and leading her back out into the hall, down through the darkness to the room with the sword.

"Exciting, no?" Bandette said. "Can you not hear the music?" Heloise could by no means hear the music. She could hear nothing but the pounding of her heart, her uncertain breaths, and . . . at least in her mind . . . an almost waterfall-like stream of sweat down her back.

"Hmm," Bandette said, flipping through the pages of the book she'd discovered. "There seem to be many tables of shipping dates, and the names of various people, and quite a scurrilous collection of crimes. It would be quite horrible, from the viewpoint of the reprehensible Monsieur Sauvage, if this book were to fall into police hands."

"Hold this, will you?" Bandette added, putting the book in Heloise's hands.

"I have discovered and memorized the code," Bandette then announced, standing in front of the keypad. "You will please now witness a master thief going about the execution of her trade." And with that, Bandette snatched a bronze spear from the wall, turned away from the number pad, and hurled it with all her might, all the way across the room.

"No," Heloise said, watching the spear's arc.

"No!" Heloise added, watching as the spear sped through the air in frozen moments, stretching forever, endless in time, heading toward the glass case with the Chinese sword, a glass case that the spear shattered, causing time to not only resume its usual pace but seemingly even to surpass it, racing forward with good speed as sirens sounded, as cries of alarm erupted not only from the nearby bedroom but also the surrounding rooms, and the hallways were bathed in the red lights of the Klaxon bells roaring so loud that Heloise could barely hear aBandette speak.

"Oh no," the thief said with a smile. "It seems I have erred."

. . . .

The guns were frightening, and time was again playing tricks on Heloise, so that it seemed it was only moments before the gangster's guards and their guns emerged into the hall, while it took Heloise eons to take two simple steps. And then there were bullets, and there was Bandette's whispered advice to *"not be where the bullets are, for they are unfriendly and antisocial,"* and the young thief was constantly tugging and pushing, moving Heloise as if she were no more than a prop. Bandette was using the sheathed sword to thunk the heads of the guards if they came too close, all the while moving Heloise this way and that, always with bullets thunking into the walls, into the floor, into the ceiling, and Bandette was continuously urging Heloise to hear the music, but for Heloise there was no music. There was nothing but the hammering of her heart and the blasting of the guns. There was nothing but her own whimpers squeaking as she and Bandette were racing down the hall, and then there was a window that was shattered by bullets and they were crashing through, with Bandette even then on her phone, calling the police (*Many shots fired! It is quite dangerous!*

Bandette reached into the safe and pulled out a small red book.

You should bring candy bars, to be safe!), and the thief was making another call (*All is well, Daniel! We shall arrive shortly!*), and then Heloise and the teen girl were landing on the lawns, Bandette without the slightest of stumbles, and Heloise with enough stumbles to make up the difference, and then there was a man who ran from the side of the house and stuck the barrel of his gun into Bandette's stomach.

It was a large gun.

It was a large man.

It was Gilles Sauvage, with his scars and his muscles, his dark eyes and his sneering mouth, with his long list of crimes that the police had never been able to prove, and of course . . . still with that very large gun.

"Ahh, here is the dog," Bandette said, looking down at the gun that was pressing into the red of her costume. Heloise began screaming, already hearing . . . in her mind . . . the sharp report of the gun, the sickening sound of impact, of . . . of . . .

"The *dog*?" she said. What did Bandette mean?

"The *dog*?" Gilles echoed, looking down at his gun, his finger tightening on the trigger, but his expression was uncertain, because it was true that he had just woken from sleep, and perhaps he was dreaming, because where had this brightly colored waif come from, and what was she saying about—

It was at that moment that the German shepherd bit deep into the backside of the city's most notorious criminal.

It was at that moment that the German shepherd, who had earlier been embraced in Bandette's hug, bit deep into the backside of the city's most notorious criminal, a man who let out a very high-pitched scream, a screech heard even over and above the Klaxons and sirens that were still sounding, dropping his pistol in his pain and shock.

"Good dog," Bandette said, bending down to once more scratch the dog beneath his chin, which was a bit of a challenge, owing to how it was still enthusiastically biting and chomping on a crime lord's bottom.

"Ahh, the weapon," Bandette said. "You will hold this, no?" The thief picked up the fallen pistol and handed it to Heloise, who was too dumbfounded to do anything but clutch it to her chest along with the book Bandette had discovered in the criminal's safe.

"Now we should scamper," Bandette said. "As if we were thieves. Which we are. Which is marvelous. Can you yet hear the music?"

Heloise could not. It was still just the Klaxons, and still just the bullets flying, as the guards emerged from the house and were firing on them even as they were crawling back over the property's wall, a skip and a dance for Bandette but

a horrible chore for Heloise, who needed to be pushed and prodded and who shrieked as she fell over the top to the sidewalk on the other side and who was nearly run down by a motor scooter whooshing to a stop, tires squealing.

Heloise, her seat planted on the sidewalk, looked up to see Daniel astride the scooter. He was one of Bandette's urchins . . . perhaps her boyfriend . . . the boy who made deliveries for a Thai restaurant and seemed forever confused but always quite happy, and most often smelling of peanut sauce.

"Ahh, Daniel," Bandette said. "You have arrived precisely on time and have perhaps earned a kiss, or possibly even a candy bar, should either of the two be available in sufficient supply. Have you brought what I requested?"

"Yes," he said, reaching into the rear saddlebags where he carried his delivery boxes of noodles even as Heloise was desperately trying to get onto the scooter, for surely it had arrived for use as an escape vehicle?

But, no, Bandette was gently pushing her back, and she was placing the sword on the sidewalk, and she was whispering instructions to the police-woman even as Daniel thrust a bundle of clothing into Heloise's hands, a bundle that was . . . her police uniform?

"Quickly, Heloise," Bandette said, gesturing to the clothes.

"Quickly, Daniel," Bandette said, standing upright on the back of the scooter even as Daniel sped away, even as the thief waved to Heloise, leaving her behind

• • • • • • • • • • • • • • • • • • • •

It was only four minutes later that B. D. Belgique of the Special Police Forces arrived on the scene with a contingent of well-armed police, striding from an armored van with his cigarette in place and his curses already spewing, only to encounter the first officer on the scene, who was, of course, Heloise.

"What are you doing here?" he asked between barking orders at the men and women who were swarming from the arriving vehicles.

"I heard the call and investigated," Heloise said, smoothing her police uniform, which was somewhat tight, owing to the black bodysuit beneath.

"You investigated?" Belgique growled. "That's not your place, and it's too dangerous! Don't you know whose house this is? Gilles Sauvage! He's . . . he's . . ."

The detective paused.

His cigarette, in an unheard-of incident, fell from his mouth.

"Is that . . . the Chinese sword?" he said. His voice was almost a whisper. So strange to hear him speaking so low.

"It is," Heloise said. "And *this* is a notebook filled with evidence of the theft, and of hundreds of other crimes, and *this* is Sauvage's pistol, recently fired, and I believe if we match the bullets we will find it was used in many crimes." Belgique accepted these gifts with wide eyes, with eyes growing ever wider, with eyes that kept staring to the sword on the sidewalk, and also to the policewoman standing in front of him, all the while with the acrid scent of the cigarette billowing up from below, the officers swarming through gates they'd never before been able to breach, held back by the laws of the city, but now . . . with these reports of gunfire . . . they were streaming inside.

"You've solved the case of the Chinese sword," Belgique said. His strength was returning. His air of command was swelling. But there was something else, as well.

A warmth.

"I have," Heloise said, surprised at her own brashness. "You can repay me by promising that, whenever you're at my apartment, you will not smoke." The air around Heloise was different from before, lighter, sweeter, more fluid, always moving, and . . . and . . . there was music. Heloise could hear it. Bandette was right. The thief was correct.

There was music.

B. D. Belgique of the Special Police Forces bent over and clutched at the Chinese sword, picking it up, taking a deep breath, a long exhalation, and Heloise could see the smallest of smiles on the man with the big nose.

"It's a promise," Belgique said. "I will not smoke in your apartment. But . . . why would I ever even go to your apartment?"

"Ahh," Heloise said. "That is *your* question to answer, not mine."

She wondered what would happen if she simply stepped forward and hugged him, but it was too soon, perhaps, for that. ❖

The air around Heloise was different from before, lighter, sweeter, more fluid, always moving, and there was music.

Portrait of a Muse

By Paul Tobin with Colleen Coover

Photo of Suzanne Valadon.

One of the main inspirations for the *House of the Green Mask* story line was the life of the painter and model Suzanne Valadon. I've been fascinated by her life for well over a decade, after coming across so many mentions of her when I was studying the lives of the impressionist artists. Here was a woman who modeled for such luminaries as Renoir, Pierre Puvis de Chavannes, Steinlen, and Toulouse-Lautrec. Here was a woman who was herself a great painter and who . . . in 1894 . . . became the first woman ever admitted to the Société Nationale des Beaux-Arts. Here was a woman who counted Renoir, Toulouse-Lautrec, and Degas among her mentors.

Suzanne Valadon in Toulouse-Lautrec's *Hangover: The Drinker* (1888).

Important life points for Suzanne Valadon:

- Lived (and lived well) from 1865 to 1938
- Was the daughter of an unmarried laundress
- Was a circus performer until injuring her back at fifteen after falling from a trapeze
- Used modeling not only as income but also as a means to an informal art education
- Hung out with the artistic crowd at Le Chat Noir and Au Lapin Agile. A bit of a party girl!
- Mother of cityscape artist Maurice Utrillo

Dance at Bougival (1883) by Pierre August Renoir. Valadon modeled for this painting.

Portrait of Suzanne Valadon (ca. 1880s–90s) by Théophile-Alexandre Steinlen, the artist who created the famous black cat poster for Le Chat Noir café.

La tournée du Chat noir de Rodolphe Salis (1896) by Théophile-Alexandre Steinlen.

And now, let's talk *scandal*, because scandal is . . . of course . . . the art of life. And Suzanne Valadon was certainly scandalous, especially for her day. She had an affair with Renoir. She likely had an affair with Puvis de Chavannes. She had a romance with Miguel Utrillo, a Spanish painter who was a denizen of Montmartre and its culture. Miguel is likely the father of Suzanne's son, Maurice Utrillo, but (scandal!) the true paternity is actually unknown. There was a relationship with Erik Satie, the (now) famous avant-garde composer and (*uncomfortable* scandal!) friend of Miguel Utrillo. Satie slumped around Montmartre in the late 1880s, writing avant-garde music (which is actually very pretty) and playing piano at Le Chat Noir. Poor Satie fell obsessively in love with Valadon and was crushed when she dumped him after six months. She is believed to have been his only intimate partner. *Dang*, Satie! Move on!

Self-Portrait (1898) by Suzanne Valadon.

Portrait of Erik Satie (1892) by Valadon.

Maurice Utrillo Playing with a Sling Shot (1895) by Valadon.

Valadon, of course, had no trouble moving on. There was Paul Moussis, the Montmartre stockbroker, to whom Valadon was married from 1896 until (scandal!) their divorce in 1910. And then (scandal!) there was André Utter, a friend of her *son's*, whom she romanced in 1909 when she was still married to Paul Moussis, and then married several years later in 1914. The two were separated in the 1930s.

But what does all this mean to Bandette and the House of the Green Mask? Well, I was thinking one day of Valadon, and thinking of how my studiomates at Helioscope give me and each other gifts of small drawings, etc., and then thinking in terms of a woman like Valadon, receiving her gifts of paintings from Renoir, drawings from Degas, music scores from Satie, poster sketches from Steinlen, and the odd little drawings from the odd little man, Toulouse-Lautrec. What a treasure trove! And what other riches was she amassing? It sent my head spinning, and it became one of the many inspirations for *The House of the Green Mask*, which I hope will serve as its own treasure for everyone who picks up a copy, and I'm also glad to give this tip of the hat to the grand artist Suzanne Valadon!

(Bonus for close readers: if you go back through the earlier stories, you can find Valadon paintings either being stolen by Bandette or in her various secret headquarters!)

Casting the Net (1914) by Valadon. In a later still life, *The Violin Case*, the bottom of this painting serves as a backdrop.

Raminou Sitting on a Cloth (1920) by Valadon.

View from My Window in Genets (1922) by Valadon.

The Blue Room (1923) by Valadon.

Here's me (Paul Tobin) in the gardens behind the Musée de Montmartre. Valadon and Utrillo's windows looked out over this space. Photo by Colleen Coover.

The Violin Case (1923) by Valadon. The legs of the *Casting the Net* guys are in the background.

Entrance to the Musée de Montmartre in 2008. The three-hundred-year-old building was home to many artists and writers, including Renoir, Valadon, and Utrillo. Visitors today can visit Valadon's studio, which was renovated in 2014. Photo by Colleen Coover.

CHARACTER & COVER DESIGN

Notes by Colleen Coover

A lot of new characters were introduced in this volume of *Bandette*! The dancer Abagail's style and figure are based on those of French actress and singer Brigitte Bardot, though I chose not to give her Bardot's fair hair and skin tone.

Dart Petite's pixie look is directly inspired by the 1960s British fashion icon Twiggy!

Boxley

Braden and Boxley

Cassandra, Third Daughter
of the Moon's Full Eye

Gabriella Franchester

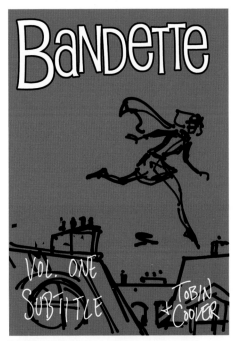

Volume 1

Volume 2, version 1

Volume 2, version 2

Volume 2, version 3

For the first volume of *Bandette*, once I hit upon the idea of having a bright, monochromatic cover, the rest of the design sort of fell into place. For volume 2, my first go was too similar to volume 1, my second try was just okay, and the third time was the charm!

Volume 3, version 1

Volume 3, version 3

Volume 3, version 2

The House of the Green Mask's story line made it a bit darker than the previous volumes, and I wanted its cover to reflect that, but my first two sketches were too quiet!